A GLIMPSE OF INFINITY

A GLIMPSE OF INFINITY

THE REALMS OF TARTARUS, BOOK THREE

BRIAN STABLEFORD

THE BORGO PRESS
MMXIII

A GLIMPSE OF INFINITY

FIRST BORGO PRESS EDITION

Published by Wildside Press LLC

www.wildsidebooks.com

ACKNOWLEDGMENT

I am greatly obliged to Heather Datta for her great kindness and consummate efficiency in scanning the text of the first edition of this novel, thus enabling me to get it back into print.

A GLIMPSE OF INFINITY

A GLIMPSE OF INFINITY

1.

In Euchronia, arrest was only a state of mind. There were no prisons. Limitation by confinement was quite unnecessary, because there was nowhere in the world that a man might hide. There was no way to keep secrets within the machine that was host to mankind. There was, of course, escape, but not within the world—only without. In Sanctuary, or in the Underworld, there was no arrest. But in Euchronia, once a man was labeled "arrested," arrested he was. Joth Magner accepted his arrest, signifying that he wanted to cooperate to the full with those who had so designated him. He took up temporary residence in the headquarters of the Euchronian Movement, in order to make himself available for consultation and interrogation, face to face. There was no real need, because he would have been available anywhere in the world *via* the screens, but that was the way he wanted it. He wanted to force his physical presence upon the Councilors who wanted his information. He wanted to be free to use all the power of his personality in his arguments.

Eliot Rypeck and Enzo Ulicon, who became his interrogators primarily because they were interested in hearing what he had to say, unlike the majority of their colleagues, were opposed to direct confrontation. They had adapted themselves, mind and body, to the mediation of machines.

In addition, they found Joth physically repellent by virtue of the fact that his face was half-metal. Nevertheless, they concurred. They felt that what Joth knew was important, and they wanted to know.

2.

"Why did you decide to follow Burstone in the first place?" asked Rypeck.

"I wanted to find out what happened to my brother. He knew about Burstone. When he went into the Underworld it was by the route that Burstone used."

"And what happened?"

"I followed him down into the lowest levels. He used a cage attached to winding gear in order to go down from the floor of the Overworld to the surface. I waited for him to come back. When he left, I went down myself. I had to see. I hadn't expected the lights—the stars—beneath the platform. But someone—maybe Burstone—wound the cage back up. I was trapped." Joth fired these sentences quickly, wanting to race ahead, to get to the arguments he wanted to put, the information that was vital. But he knew that the whole story had to be told, in order to provide a context for his arguments. These people were not merely ignorant, but misled. They had to be guided to understanding. It could not be thrust upon them.

"You don't know what Burstone was doing in the Underworld?" put in Ulicon.

"I know," said Joth. "I didn't see him, but I know. He was taking knives and tools and books, to give to the Underworlders."

"Why?"

"Ask him."

"Carry on," said Rypeck. "What happened next?"

"I panicked. I was suddenly completely afraid. Drowning in fear. Not logical. It was like stepping straight into a drug experience. Everything twisted in my mind. I couldn't think, couldn't even use my senses. I ran. Anywhere...nowhere. I ran. I fell, and when I got up I ran again. I lost contact with time. And then I ran straight into a man."

"Wait," said Rypeck. "This is one thing that we *must* have clear. A man, you say. A *human* being."

"So far as I could tell," said Joth, "he was as human as you or I. He was a savage, but he was a man. But there were others— chasing him, I think. He picked me up, and he made sure that they saw me. They were terrified, because of my face. He got away from them. But he wasn't terrified—*he knew what I was.* That's important. He knew that I was a man despite the face. He knew I came from the Overworld. You must realize that although he was a savage he wasn't ignorant. He knew what he was doing when he used me as a scarecrow to buy him time."

"And the others?" prompted Rypeck.

"This is the hard part," said Joth. "They were men, too. But they weren't like you or me. They were small and strange. Randal Harkanter had one in a cage, but that was wrong. What Harkanter had wasn't an animal, it was a man."

"Soron said that it was a rat," said Ulicon—not making an assertion, but putting the idea forward so that Joth had to react.

"What's a rat?" said Joth. "Have you ever seen one? Maybe they still exist—more likely they don't. Soron has nothing on which to base his identification except information from the prehistoric past. His opinion means nothing."

"He's an expert in his field," said Ulicon mildly.

"That's nonsense," Joth told him. "He's an expert in a field that's ten thousand years out of date. He knows *nothing* about life in the Underworld as it really is. Do you really think that a man can walk into a new world, armed with knowledge which pertains to circumstances as they were ten millennia ago, and make meaningful judgments about the nature of that world? Do you think that there is any way that Soron possibly *could* know anything?"

"We take the point," said Rypeck. "But what do *you* know? How can you contradict what Soron said?"

"I lived with these people," said Joth. "The warriors who picked me up took me back to their village. One of them took me into his house. They looked after me while I was convinced that I was dying. They talked to me. The man, Camlak, and his daughter Nita. There was a human girl there, too—Huldi."

"You are drawing a distinction between men and humans," said Rypeck. "How?"

"There's no other way," said Joth. "There's no word we can apply to these people except men, even though they aren't truly human. They aren't animals. To call them 'rats' is to make a gross and dangerous error. They call themselves the Children of the Voice. They claim to have souls, and to be able to communicate with those souls on occasion. They speak English, although they call it Ingling. That is to say, it's a form of English. It's a language with many new words, and some words we're familiar with have been abandoned. But they read books from the Overworld. They read them, and they make some use of what they read—when they can. What else can you call someone who reads the same books that you read, speaks the same language as you do, and cares for you when you're sick? What else but a *man.* And yet they have gray fur. Their skulls are a strange and grotesque shape. Why should those things make a difference?"

Rypeck coughed, and hesitated before speaking. "In your father's book," he said, tentatively, "there are references to the people of the Underworld. Which people did he mean?"

Joth waved his hand—a brief, angry gesture. "*He didn't know.* He had no possible way of knowing. If some of what he said was true, then it was inspiration or accident. But he didn't know. You *must* understand that this has nothing to do with my father. He's dead. He may have been the trigger which began all this, but now it's something different. If you confuse what I have to say with what my father said, then we can't possibly reach any kind of an understanding."

"I'm sorry," said Ulicon, "but from our point of view what happened to your father *is* important. It could be vital. We need to know how your father knew what he did and why he thought what he did. You have no real idea of what happened when the rat or the man or whatever disappeared from Harkanter's cage.

You were there and you saw it, but it knocked you out. You were too close to the blast. That fearful burst of mental energy rocked half the world, and it *must*, in some way, be related to what your father experienced as a matter of course, in his dreams. We have to fit *all* the pieces of this jigsaw together, Joth—not just the ones you want to play."

Joth shook his head doubtfully.

"Carry on with the account of what happened to you," suggested Rypeck. "We can return to these points later."

Joth shrugged. "I don't know how long I was ill," he said, "or how long I stayed in the village afterwards. Without night and day, time became meaningless. The Underworld runs on subjective time—there are no clocks. From seconds to seasons, all intervals of time are the same to them. The only duration which means anything to them is the time it takes to get tired, or the time it takes to get hungry. Even the length of a man's life is unimportant, because no one dies of old age—there's no such thing as a lifespan. Everybody dies, when the time comes, by disease or violence.

"We—that is, the girl Huldi and I—watched one of their religious festivals—a communion of souls. I can't pretend to understand it. I wish I did. At the time, I thought I had a certain insight. Now, I'm not sure.

"There was a ritual, in which Camlak played the part of the sun, while his father—who had been the leader of his people—personified night. Camlak killed his father—executed him according to ritual—and so became the king. But the strange thing is that the ritual mimicked a different world. In their world, there is no sun, and no night. They were acting out a *mystery*, something which had meaning only within *another* world—a world which, for them, fulfills all the functions of the supernatural.

"To the Children of the Voice, the Overworld is both Heaven and Hell. It is the universe outside their own, within which their lives are sealed, and whose forces give structure and purpose and meaning to their own lives. This is completely beyond the scope of my father's book and its message. If my father, in his dreams, found some way of seeing into the Underworld, perhaps even into the minds of the people who live there, then he could not make use of what he saw. He could not understand. This makes nonsense of his ideas. We could not bring the people of the Underworld out into the light, because everything they are is identified with the darkness—it is not only their bodies which have adapted, but also their *minds*.

"You must realize that the inhabitants of the Underworld are *not like us*. They are *alien*. And yet they are men. In the Overworld we tend to have a very narrow view of humanity, and of life. We have learned to hate the men on the ground— the men who stayed on the ground in the distant past—because they did not think like Euchronians. Our history makes us hate, despite the hypocritical voice of our reason. But our history is out of date. Our attitudes are out of date. There is another world beneath our feet—and it is not the one we think it is. It is not the one my father wanted to save, *and it is not the one Heres wants to destroy.*"

Ulicon and Rypeck exchanged glances. Each suspected that Joth Magner was deranged—that his mind had been somehow twisted by his experiences. But each man was afraid of his own suspicion. Of the ten or twelve men close enough to Heres to influence the Hegemon's thinking, only these two wanted to believe that the present course of action was wrong. Joth Magner was their one hope of finding a reason which could turn Euchronia aside.

The plain fact was that from top to bottom, the entire Euchronian Movement—the authentic voice of Euchronian society—was frightened. From the moment when rediscovery of the Underworld had been forced upon them by the publicity given to Carl Magner's *Marriage of Heaven and Hell*, fear had been building up in virtually every citizen of the new world. At first, the fear had been a source of stimulation, excitement in a world which lacked excitation. Magner's absurd proposal to open the Overworld in order to allow the inhabitants of the surface to emerge into the daylight had been a fashionable distraction. But once revealed, the Underworld could not be forgotten. Magner had died for what he believed, and his death had underlined effectively the fact that something real was at stake—that the issue, once raised, could not be put away again. The rediscovery of the Underworld put all the old arguments into a new context.

Rafael Heres, with his position as Hegemon of the Movement under threat, had tried to make political capital out of Magner by making the Underworld a matter of Euchronian concern. Events had turned against him. He had tried to quell the fear by drawing its source into a second Euchronian plan, but the fear had run wild, and could not be contained. Deliberately fed by certain dissatisfied and delinquent elements in the Overworld, the Underworld had become such a bugbear that Heres had been forced to meet it head-on. Instead of recruiting it, he was committed to destroying it. To soothe the troubled mind of Euchronian society, he had undertaken to destroy a world. And Euchronia would accept nothing less. The people of the Overworld knew no way to live with uncertainty—ten thousand years of Euchronian history had made certain of that. If Heres and the Movement had no final answer, then the Movement was finished—and so, perhaps, was the Overworld. Euchronia had always claimed to be the ultimate answer. Now it had to defend its claim. Heres and the vast majority of his followers saw one answer and one only: the Underworld must be destroyed.

Rypeck and Ulicon, however, believed that there was no such simple answer. But if they were to find an alternative—or even a reason why the obvious answer was no answer at all—they had to know more about the world below the platform. Only Joth Magner could tell them. If anyone could.

3.

The convoy came to a halt at midnight. Midnight meant nothing on the road of stars, but Germont, inevitably, had carried the habits and the circadian rhythms of the Overworld with him into the realms of Tartarus.

He spoke into the microphone which connected him to the other vehicles. "We rest here for the night," he said. "No one goes outside, for any reason. Alpha-three, Beta-seven and Delta-five will maintain all-night watch using searchlights. Note anything moving, report anything dangerous, keep the lights circling. Do not open fire without orders. That's all."

The driver of the vehicle turned to look down over his shoulder at the commander of the expeditionary force. "Shall I switch off the headlights?" he asked.

"Yes," said Germont. "And douse the interior lighting as well. I'm coming up to take a look around with the searchlight." He left the communications network and hauled himself up into the cockpit of the armored car, to take the seat beside the driver.

High above—he could not estimate *how* high—the single line of electric stars ran back and forth across the solid sky, becoming a yellow blur in the distance as it faded toward the horizon.

"It really was a road," said the driver, quietly. "Ten thousand years ago. A long, straight highway running hundreds of miles. It's covered now, but it hasn't been wholly obliterated. It's an easy ride—the wheels go through this stuff like a knife. We're so heavy we must be running on the old surface itself."

"It was a road," confirmed Germont. "It's a road in the Overworld, too. When the platform was Planned, certain basic patterns were retained. This was an important road. That must be why the Planners left it lighted—after a fashion. It must have been a major access right up to the sealing of the platform."

They watched the white beam of the searchlight in the third vehicle back as it played across the terrain to the righthand side of the column. The Underworld had not reclaimed the road, but it had reclaimed the city. Even the flat, impermeable apron of the highway had been overgrown, but it had offered little enough encouragement to the fungoid life-forms which predominated here. It had been carpeted, and nothing more. But the old buildings had offered support and framework to an ecosystem which was not replete with self-supporting structures. The new life of the Underworld had found a use for cities, and it had taken over despite the poisons which often built up there. In time, even the atomic and chemical waste would be co-opted, somehow, into the cycles of life which were adapting to the corpses of civilization. The process was going on, even now. Poison is a temporary thing. It kills, but out of the death it causes there comes new life, ultimately.

This city had become a forest, its concrete bones substituting for the xylem skeletons which had been lost when the old world was condemned to darkness. All the trees were gone, but the forests simply moved into the cities. Life is never defeated—evolution simply changes gear, and the process of adaptation begins, and continues forever.

"It's all so still," said the driver. "Nothing moves at all."

"There's no wind," said Germont. "Not here. There must be air currents down here, and fierce ones where the situation is right. But here the air's quite dead. Stale."

"There are no animals," said the driver. "None at all."

Germont shrugged. "They won't wait for the light. They must have been able to hear the convoy for miles."

"But why would they run?" asked the driver. "They sure as hell haven't learned to be afraid of armored trucks."

"They'd be afraid of the noise," said Germont.

The driver shook his head. "I don't like it," he said. "That line of lights in the sky, these great hulking masses of sponge on either side. It feels as though there's something different about just *here*. It's as if that stuff out there was *full* of things just sitting on either side of the road but staying clear. Watching us."

For a few moments, Germont didn't reply. His eyes followed

the cone of light swinging across the face of the forest. Then he said: "Get some sleep."

As the driver clambered down from the cockpit and moved back to the belly of the vehicle, where eight other men were waiting—resting, talking, peeping through the portholes, and trying to hold down the unease in their stomachs, Germont continued to follow the progress of the light.

All the plant flesh was gray. There were all shades, but no colors. This was a color-blind world. Even in the lands where the stars were clustered in the sky, Germont thought, the light would be dim enough to rob ordinary human vision of color perception and depth perception. But what about the men who lived here? Perhaps they could see colors. Perhaps not the same colors as the men of the Overworld.

The most noticeable feature of the plant masses which dressed each of the broken hulks that had once been human habitations was their corporateness. Every one consisted of thousands—perhaps millions—of individuals, and the range of specific types was considerable. And yet all the grays and whites and blacks were *blurred.* The whole structure was amorphous. All the individual cups and caps, bulbs and wracks, squabs and sacs, were *integrated*, making use of one another, intertwining with one another, almost blending with one another. Germont knew that the apparent corporate identity was an illusion—that there must be fierce competition, interspecific and intraspecific, for every inch of support and space—but he was not sure that the illusion might not be more real than the reality. The competition *was* collaboration, of a kind. The vast tangle of shapes, crinose and petinated, aciform and orbicular, *was*—in some way—a unit. Out of the internal balance of the struggle for existence there was made some kind of entity. The whole forest, which might stretch for ten or fifty miles back on either side of the road, was a colossal life-system, a superorganism. The city had come to life. And the convoy—forty-five vehicles in single file carrying five hundred men to inoculate a whole world with death—was just a worm in its gut. A dangerous invader inside it, waiting to bite.

Germont's vehicle was air-tight and armored. Its six huge wheels could cope with virtually any terrain. It carried a flame-thrower and a machine gun in the turret where the searchlight was mounted. It was a sealed package containing a fragment of the Overworld. Nothing could possibly harm him, or any of his men. They could spew out poison to eat up the life of the Underworld's cities, but the Underworld could do nothing to them.

And yet Germont was afraid.

He came down from the cockpit, seated himself in front of the miniature holoscreen at his communications console, and activated it. Some minutes passed before his call was answered. He did not know the woman who answered, and he did not ask her name. She represented the Movement, and that was identity enough so far as Germont was concerned.

He gave exact details of the convoy's position and confirmed that he was exactly on schedule.

"The Delta contingent will remain in this locale," he said. "They will make preliminary investigations in the morning. Preparations for experimental seeding will take place as per schedule. We have encountered no difficulties. The other three contingents will proceed to the rendezvous with Zuvara at nine A.M. We have seen no sign of any animal life-form. All equipment is functioning, and air filtration is one hundred percent effective. Water purification apparatus has not yet been tested in the field, but contingent Delta will report tomorrow."

The woman acknowledged the information, and Germont switched off. There was no conversation. The woman's presence had been a formality—a concession to the principle of human involvement. The cybernet had recorded his report, and would have acted on it had any action been necessary. It would also have relayed any new instructions. The illusion of human communication was in some ways similar to the illusion of unity in the forest life-system. At the most basic level, no such communication was taking place. But the purpose of human communication was what gave the perfect arbitration of the cybernet a meaning.

He went back into the belly of the vehicle, and lay on his bunk waiting for sleep. He found difficulty in relinquishing his tight hold on consciousness, and when he finally slept, he dreamed.

More than once, during the long night, he awoke into his dreams. And what he found there frightened him.

4.

"Why didn't you come back to the Overworld when you had the opportunity?" asked Rypeck.

Joth put the tips of his fingers to his mouth and pressed his palms together while he contemplated the question.

"The reasons are complicated," he said, finally. "They didn't seem so at the time, but I didn't think about it much. I just did what I felt I ought to do. I suppose I worked out the reasons subconsciously—or perhaps I invented them later to explain myself. When I found the door in the metal wall, I found my father. He'd finally been compelled to look outside his night-mares, into the substance of his visions. He'd found a way into the world he wanted to save, just as I'd found a way out. We collided. It wasn't really that much of a coincidence—the same things which moved him moved me, factors external to both of us.

"He wasn't quite dead when I found him, but he couldn't do or say anything. He was still bleeding from a wound—a bullet wound. Finding him there just knocked the bottom out of the world. I was running home, and suddenly there was no home to run to. By then I had other priorities. Nita and Huldi were cut adrift, just as I was. When I buried my father I felt myself thrown back into their predicament. Drifting in the world, with no purpose—cut right out of the cloth of existence. Whether I came back or stayed, I'd have had to start all over again. I stayed, because that's where I was. I stayed with them.

"I fell ill again. I just didn't have the constitution to live down there. They had to cut some parasites out of my back and the wound wouldn't heal. I got worse. Then we met the hellkin. He joined us. His name was...is...Iorga."

Joth paused, expecting some reaction.

"This is the...man...who killed Harkanter?" asked Ulicon, filling the pause.

"He had to," said Joth.

"Let's not leap forward now," said Rypeck, with a hint of impatience in his voice. "We'll leave the matter of judgment until the proper time. Tell us what happened."

"Iorga had seen Camlak, with another man from the village. We went back toward the wall. We found the other, but not Camlak. Camlak had been shot, by the man called Soron. He had come out into the open because Harkanter was trapped in a mud hole. He wanted to help. The other—Chemec—had been more cautious, and had stayed hidden. But Camlak didn't think there was anything to be afraid of. That was my fault. It was because of me that Camlak wasn't afraid. But they shot him."

"Harkanter claimed that he was attacked—that the rat had a knife." This interjection came from Ulicon.

Joth shook his head.

"There was a misunderstanding," said Rypeck.

"I had to get him back," said Joth, ignoring the remark. "It was up to me. He kept me alive in the village. But for him I'd be dead. If not for me, he wouldn't have been at the wall. He wouldn't have tried to help Harkanter. I came up to the Overworld to bring him back. I brought Iorga with me to help."

"Why come back in secret?" demanded Rypeck. "Why come to steal the rat? Why break into Harkanter's house with guns?"

"Do you honestly think," said Joth, "that anyone would have listened to me? Was there any other way? The one thing I wanted to do, at that time, was free Camlak. I had no other purpose. I set about doing it in the only way it could be done— by stealth. We didn't intend to kill anyone—we just wanted to take Camlak off Harkanter and back to the Underworld. When that was done, I intended to come back for the explanations. I had myself patched up by a doctor, and then Julea got Harkanter to open his door to us. It would have gone according to plan. We went down into the cellars. Camlak was in a cage. I saw him there. And then there was an explosion inside my head."

There was a brief silence. This was the climactic point. They all knew that this was the fulcrum of the whole matter, but none of them knew how to approach it.

Eventually, it was Ulicon who spoke.

"I was sitting in an armchair," he said. "I was reading some printouts. It was as if I'd been stabbed in the back of my neck, the blade traveling upwards into my brain. I couldn't hold the pages—I just lost control of my hands and they shook like leaves in a high wind. My eyes were closed, but I was *seeing*. The light—or the illusion of light—was almost unbearably bright. Images flashed in an incoherent sequence. It was all too bright and too fast for me to make sense of it, but some of the images I could almost focus, and recall. What I saw was a confused conglomerate of visual memories. I looked—through someone or something else's eyes—into the Underworld. I saw what your father saw. It took time, but I came to realize that what had happened to me—and hundreds of thousands of others—was no more than what had already happened to your father. With him, it took years; with us, less than a second. He, perhaps, saw through many pairs of eyes, had access to millions of memories. We saw through one pair of eyes one set of visual images.

"For a while, when I found that these alien memories were imprinted in my mind, I feared that I would go mad. Perhaps, by the standards which were mine a few days ago, I am no longer sane. If so, that is true of fully half the members of our society. Our minds have been invaded. We have memories that are not our own. When we wake, we are constantly aware, but at least we are in control. When we sleep....

"The citizens of Euchronia have no nightmares. That is the way it was intended to be. Euchronia was intended to be the answer to intellectual unrest. But that is no longer true. We now know that our minds are open. Perhaps we have opened them ourselves—we do not know. But in any case, our inner being can no longer be entirely our own. Our inner space is no longer delimited by the confines of our physical being. We wonder, now, if any one of us can speak of *my* self, *my* mind.

"We now understand *The Marriage of Heaven and Hell*, and why your father wrote it. We think that we understand how the alien ideas coming into his mind comingled and integrated with his own. We now have nightmares, as he did. Some of us—I don't know how many—now catch, as he did, the leakage of other minds while we sleep. The mindblast has ripped away the shielding around our selves, and we are no longer secure.

"We know that the focus of the blast was Harkanter's house. We know that the being in the cage disappeared, and we can only believe that its disappearance was the cause of the blast. We live in desperate fear of this incessant pollution of ourselves which is coming from the Underworld. Our reflex action is to destroy— to obliterate the minds which are invading our personal space. What Eliot and I fear is that the destruction of the Underworld is not a real solution to the problem. We fear that the clock cannot be turned back, and that our minds are permanently altered. What we fear is that in destroying the Underworld we may destroy our chance to find a *real* answer. There are only two people in the world who might help us find such an answer. You are one. You must tell me *everything* that you know or suspect about what happened in Harkanter's cellar."

"I thought that he'd destroyed himself," said Joth, slowly. "I saw him—my eyes were actually upon him in the moment he disappeared. But Nita believes that he is alive. Elsewhere. She spoke about her soul—the festival I saw in the village was called the Communion of Souls. She said that during such a communion she had looked into other worlds, and that her father had gone into one. But the festival was just a ritual—it was a mime. Nothing happened that I was aware of. There must have been so much more—so much that I couldn't begin to know.

"Camlak's memories came into their minds too, but they just

accepted it. They weren't even surprised. Perhaps it happens all the time, to them. But I don't think so. I think there's something about the way they live and think that we can never understand—something that is utterly different from us. And yet there's so much that is the same....

"*I don't know what happened.* What you've said may all be true. It seems reasonable. But all I know is what you know—that Camlak's memories have been blasted into my mind and your mind and many other minds. It could happen again. It probably will. Everything that you and the whole Movement fears could come true. Our minds might be dissolved inside our heads. But there's one thing that you must consider. Nita and Chemec weren't surprised. They *knew* what had happened. And if they, and the Children of the Voice as a whole, really know and understand what happened, then they can do it again. If you try to exterminate the Children of the Voice, then they may react as Camlak reacted when Harkanter put him in a cage. If you start a war with the people of the Underworld, you might lose. They can destroy you."

5.

Abram Ravelvent was tired. Since he had become tangled in this affair through acquaintance with Carl Magner, it had taken years off his life. His initial interest had been mere curiosity—a typical fascination for the unusual. He had once found intellectual puzzles a source of delight. Now he was lost inside one. What had been a game had become a prison. Once, he had been able to choose where he would stand in the argument. He had committed his belief on the instruction of a whim. Now, he was completely bound up. He no longer dared to believe, or even to guess. But still people came to him with questions and arguments. He was still an "expert" to be consulted. People still looked to him for confirmation and correction. They asked nothing of him but certainty, because they so desperately wanted to know that someone, somewhere, had answers in his pocket.

Even now, he kept up the sham. He would not, could not, bring himself to relinquish the pretense that had sustained him through so many years.

But the persistent answering, when he knew no answers, made him very tired indeed.

He stared at the image of Joel Dayling which hovered above his desk. Dayling looked equally tired. His expression was grim.

"It's no longer a matter of politics." he was saying. "I no longer *have* to defeat Euchronia because Euchronia is dead. It died when its basic premise was overturned. There is no stable future. There is no secure present. It's no longer a matter of Eupsychians and Euchronians, trying to topple Heres from his pedestal. We're all in the same boat now, and the Movement is falling apart. Everyone has a voice now, not just the Movement. I'm not interested in getting Heres out of office now—I'm interested in saving the world, if it can be saved. What I want from you is an opinion, that's all. Not your vote or your endorsement. I just want to *know*—can Heres destroy the Underworld? Is it possible?"

Ravelvent didn't know. He didn't want to answer. But even while he hesitated and looked for an evasion, the rhetoric was trying to surface inside his skull. He fought, trying to keep perspective.

"Not the way the world thinks," he said. "Maybe *this* world could be destroyed with a snap of the fingers, but not the world down there. The people are used to thinking of the Overworld as one vast unit—one great big machine-wrapped family. That's their idea of what a world is. But the Underworld is very different. With our resources, perhaps we could destroy it— destroy all the higher life-forms, at any rate. But not in years, or decades, or perhaps centuries. They don't have a machine-host which can just be switched off. We'll have to go into that world and spread our poisons and our diseases mile by mile. No one in Euchronia has any idea of the true *size* of the world. We have instant electronic presence—we can go anywhere in the world by sitting in front of a screen and pressing a switch. You and I are thousands of miles apart, and yet we're face-to-face. No one understands how big the Underworld is. Not even Heres. He may destroy the Underworld, but I doubt it. You just can't conceive of the magnitude of the task that he's set himself."

"If what I've heard is true," said Dayling, "Heres' chief weapon—perhaps the only one that matters—is a virus. Rumor has it that this thing will lay waste the Underworld's plant life utterly, and that it will spread like wildfire."

"I don't know that I can comment on that," said Ravelvent.

"I'm not asking you to give away any secrets," said the Eupsychian, slightly scornfully. "Even if you know any. I'm not fishing for information I can use in a whispering campaign. I want to know just what kind of a chance Heres' present policy has of success. Treat the question hypothetically. What would be the limitations of such a virus? Can it be made, and if so, will it do what it has to?"

Ravelvent hesitated, but then carried on. He saw no point at all in concealing the truth as he saw it.

"What we know so far," he said, "suggests that the Underworld life-system is, at primary production level, almost totally derived from fungal and algal forms native to the pre-Euchronian era. If these can be successfully attacked, the bottom is knocked out of virtually every food-chain that exists down there. If the fungoids and algoids can be destroyed, animal life will cease to be possible. What Heres' scientists are trying to do is tailor a family of viruses to attack chemical structures unique to the kinds of cell which are found in the Underworld life-system, but not our own, which is derived from very different kinds of plant. This is not difficult. Fungi and algae survive in the Overworld as pests, and research to weed out such parasites using tailored viruses was going on as far back as the prehistoric ages. It was one of the first fields of research which the Movement reinstituted on the platform.

"The problems involved are twofold. In the first instance, we have no idea as to the possible reactivity of the Underworld's life-system, or its capacity for self-repair. We don't know what degree of immunity to expect, and we don't know how quickly the organisms in the Underworld will discover immunity. There is reason to believe that the Underworld's entire ecosystem is in the tachytelic evolutionary phase, which means that its capacity to absorb and withstand attack of this kind could be high.

"The second problem is transmission of the diseases. This will happen naturally, to some extent. In a given locale, the viruses will—as you put it—spread like wildfire. But introducing a disease into a life-system isn't like lighting a fuse and waiting for an explosion. Tailored diseases have difficulty in spreading simply because there's no reservoir of infection within the system as a whole. There is no such thing as an unlimited epidemic. These viruses are going to have to be assisted in their conquest by constant seeding over very wide areas. That will take a great deal of time and a tremendous level of production. A great deal of effort goes into the isolation of one gram of a crystalline virus. When we talk of destroying worlds, we talk in tons rather than grams.

"The viruses may do what Heres thinks is necessary, but it won't be done overnight, and the amount of resistance within the life-system may be far greater than we hope. And in the meantime—while Heres' grand plan is in progress—new factors may enter the situation. Anything might happen. Heres may have picked the simple answer, but it isn't an easy one. There are no easy ones."

"Thanks," said Dayling. "That's what we needed to know."

"We?" queried Ravelvent.

"Don't worry. We aren't a revolutionary movement. Not anymore. We don't have to be. The revolution started without us. Now, we're the government-in-reserve. When Heres reaches the end of his rope, the Council will have to turn to someone. We intend to be the only people with ideas. If you want a job, Abram, you only have to ask."

Ravelvent laughed shortly.

"You always wanted to be dictator," he said, with a hint of bitterness.

"Not at all," said Dayling. "I always wanted to be messiah."

6.

"Did you see *anything* which suggested that the rats are telepathic?" demanded Rypeck.

"They're not rats," said Joth.

"Do they use telepathy?" persisted Rypeck.

Joth shook his head. "Camlak said nothing to suggest that they could. But afterwards...Nita knew what had happened. Maybe they have telepathy but don't use it. I don't know."

"They have it," said Ulicon, quickly. "We *know* that. Memory images can be transmitted and implanted. What Joth's evidence suggests is that they can't control it. In all probability, they're not even aware of it. They take for granted the fact that their minds *spill over* from their selves, that there's some kind of unitary organization within the species—perhaps like a hive of bees. This property of their minds is completely bound up with ritual and religion—to them, it's natural. They personify the collective as their souls. The communion of souls is a social thing, where the whole social unit shares some experience through invoking this group identity."

Rypeck waved a hand angrily. "It doesn't even *begin* to look like an explanation," he said. "Enzo, we must do better than this. You can't use this garbled nonsense to explain the fact that the rat—or man, or whatever—*disappeared* from that cage. Where did it go? Did it dissipate itself into your hypothetical superorganism? What happened to its *body*? We mustn't lose sight of the fact that we're dealing with a *physical event*. The blast of energy was the result of the *physical* phenomenon. The mental side effect was just that—a *side effect*. We mustn't fall into the trap of thinking that the transmission of memories from the rat to everyone within receiving distance was the purpose of what happened. It wasn't. It was, in all likelihood, quite accidental. The wave which carried the information is what we should be interested in, and that wave was generated by what we would previously have considered to be an impossible event. The very fact that the intensity of what we *felt* seems to have depended more or less on the inverse square of the distance between ourselves and the focal point surely suggests that we are dealing with a physical phenomenon whose psychical effects are really secondary."

"That kind of division doesn't make sense," said Ulicon.

"Enzo, we communicate *via* electromagnetic radiation. We speak into a microphone, and at the other end, someone hears our words. The information is in one brain, which translates thought into sound. The microphone translates sound into electricity. The electricity is translated into modified radio waves, which are translated back into electricity, back into sound, and then back into information in another brain. We can't try to understand such a process by what goes on in the brains, and *only* what goes on in the brains. Is that telepathy? Of course it is—information is transmitted from brain to brain. But in order to understand it we must understand the physics of it. We can't consider it simply as a psychic phenomenon. To do so makes nonsense of it."

"All right," said Ulicon. "So it's a problem in physics. So what?"

"We've already established," said Rypeck, "that the Children of the Voice don't *use* telepathy. What does that mean? It means that they aren't normally able to translate ideas into a form which can be carried by the kind of energy which is involved in the event we're trying to understand. It's as though they were mute—unable to translate ideas into sounds so that they can be transmitted from one brain to another. This failure could be at one of several levels. They might lack the physical apparatus for so doing—as if they had no tongues. Or they might lack the coding capacity—that is to say, they have the tongues but not the language. Or they might lack the power—as if they couldn't expel the breath through the throat in order to vibrate the vocal cords Any of these might be true. But what we must do is abandon the notion that there is something magical or supernatural about what happened, or about the kind of thing we have to deal with. We may have to introduce a whole new physics into our scientific understanding, but what we must not do is try to make do with a whole new metaphysics."

"All that may be true," complained Joth, "but it doesn't help. You both seem obsessed with trying to find words to describe what happened. But that isn't going to stop Heres destroying the Children of the Voice. He must be prevented from committing genocide. Isn't that what we're here for? Isn't *that* what we're trying to do. It's what *I'm* trying to do."

"It's not so simple," said Rypeck.

"It's simple enough," said Joth. "It's saving millions of people from being wiped out because Heres and the Euchronians are scared. If they had been reasonable in the first place—if they'd only been prepared to recognize the fact that there *are* people in the Underworld who should be dealt with as people—then this whole thing wouldn't have happened."

"We cannot simply wait," said Rypeck. "As Heres and millions of others see it—as Enzo and I see it, even—our minds and our identities are threatened with destruction. We know that it could be done. We want to see that it isn't. If the threat is not to be faced in Heres' way—a way which we and others consider to be extremely dangerous—then we must find another way to face it. If we are not to attack the threat at its source, then we must find a defense. That logic may be hard, but it is more appropriate than the ethical logic which you are trying to apply. If Enzo and myself are prepared to hear your case and support you, it is because we are afraid that Heres' plan may precipitate the destruction it attempts to forestall, not because we want to save the Children of the Voice."

Joth felt stricken. "When I was injured," he said, in a very low voice, "my father fought for my life. He defended me against a medical committee which wanted to put me out of my supposed misery. My father won, and I have a face of steel and plastic. I was allowed to live. Sometimes, it has occurred to me to doubt whether or not my father did the right thing. I believed that the whole argument was one of ethics. After all, this is the Euchronian Millennium—the end-point of human ambition. And when my father wrote his book—I thought the argument then was a matter of ethics.

It occurs to me to wonder now—who *did* shoot my father? Who ordered it done?"

"Your father was killed by a man named Simkin Cinner," said Ulicon, gently. "No one ordered it done. And you must see that whether you approve of our motives or not, the only way of getting what you want is our way. The only way that the people of the Underworld will be allowed to live is by our proving that the Overworld has nothing to fear from them."

Joth looked him in the face, deliberately staring with his cold, metallic eyes. Ulicon could not meet the stare. No one could.

"I don't think you can prove that," said Joth. "Because you'll always be afraid. The Euchronians have always thought that the world was theirs, because of the platform and the Plan. But now we know that it's not true. The world belongs to the people of the Underworld. The Underworld *is* the world. Euchronia is a gigantic castle in the air. A dream. I think that if the Movement tries to destroy the Underworld, the Underworld will destroy the Movement, and the Overworld with it."

"That," said Rypeck, "is exactly what we fear."

7.

The driver screamed, and the armored truck swerved to the left. There was a soft sound as the nearside wing sheared fungus, and then a harsher grating noise as the metal met something more solid. The vehicle came back off the wall into the road, its nose swinging as the driver jerked the wheel.

Germont was into the cockpit in a matter of seconds. By the

glare of the headlights he could see something—someone—trying desperately to get out of the path of the vehicle. The driver had not hit the brakes.

It was too late. The truck hit the running figure and ran over the crushed body. Germont grabbed the wheel and held it steady, holding the vehicle on course. Finally, belatedly, the driver found the brake pedal with his foot, and the truck slowed to a halt.

"What the hell do you think you're doing?" demanded Germont.

"He threw something!" gasped the driver, who was shaking like a leaf. "The lights just picked him up, and he threw a rock. It hit the canopy just in front of me—I thought it was coming through. I couldn't help it."

The transparent plastic had taken the blow comfortably—there was no mark. The driver had been startled rather than scared. But the shock had been considerable.

"Cut the engine," said Germont curtly, and then turned to call to the men in the back: "Get on that searchlight! And the gun."

He dropped back to snatch up the microphone by which he could broadcast to the convoy.

"Hold your positions," he said. "Alpha-two, do you see what we ran over?"

"I see it," came the reply. "I can't make it out. Could be human. Do you want me to send someone out for a closer look?"

"No! No one gets out. Can you maneuver to get the body into the light from your headlights? I want all searchlights on. Scan the forest."

"Jacob," said the driver, speaking with unnatural quietness now that he was past the shock. "The road ahead. There used to be a cutting. The land's slipped. It's blocked. We'll have to go back and around."

Germont, with the microphone still in his hand, climbed up to a position from which he could look out of the cockpit. The light of the many searchlights showed that the forest was banked unnaturally high on either side of them. The road ran through a long, shallow canyon. The obstruction in front was steep, but it did not seem impassable.

"We can climb that," said Germont. "We don't need a road. This thing is built to hold a slope."

Somewhere back along the line, a machine gun came to life. Almost immediately, searchlight beams converged, and Germont looked back to where tiny white figures were moving on the ridge, while the bullets tore fungal tissue to pieces all around them. The soft, pulpy flesh *splashed* as the bullets hit, and sections of leathery algal frondescence fluttered in the air and writhed as they slid down the slope, robbed of their support. One of the figures was hurled back, and another. Dead and alive alike, they disappeared as great clouds of spore dust poured from the afflicted area.

There was a series of dull thuds as rocks hit the plating of Germont's vehicle. He looked up, trying to locate the throwers, while the searchlight veered back and forth.

"Stop firing!" he commanded. "They can't hurt us!"

Then the land somewhere in the rear began to slide. It was the spot where the firing had been concentrated—the bullets had weakened the ancient structure which supported the forest, and it was tumbling, sliding down into the road.

Realizing the danger, the trucks which were in the path of the slide came forward in a hurry. The first two or three managed to get far enough. One or two didn't, and the loose rock, moving with fluid smoothness, washed into them, turned them, shoved them and began to bury them. One was turned over on its side.

When the slide was over, six vehicles were trapped. Two were breached, and all had some degree of internal damage.

Angrily, Germont ordered men out of the other trucks to begin digging out the trapped men and freeing the vehicles. They came out in closed-environment suits, and for every two or three men to dig, there had to be one with a rifle. The searchlights continued to scan the slopes for signs of the attackers.

Germont went out himself, to look at the corpse which lay

in the roadway between his vehicle and the second in line. He waited while one of the doctors inspected the body.

"Is it human?" he asked, when the examination was over.

"Near enough," said the doctor.

"He must have been crazy," said Germont. "Coming at the truck like that."

"It's not a he," said the doctor. "It's a she." Then the arrow hit him. It went through the plastic suit like paper, between his ribs and deep into his chest. He died instantly.

8.

Elsewhere in the Underworld, the men from Euchronia were building a city: a city of hemispherical domes and cylindrical tunnels. The encampment beneath the plexus which had been established by Randal Harkanter and the party which he had led into the Underworld had been packed up and removed to the surface, only to be replaced by a much larger and much better equipped invasion force, whose purpose was to begin seeding the Swithering Waste with the Overworld's various biological agents of destruction, and to observe the effects thereof. It was one of several such stations—Germont's convoy was intended to establish three more—set up in a number of rather different habitats.

The seeding was done from the air, the viruses being laid out along long lines radiating like spokes from the circular metal wall which was the base of the plexus. The "electronic bats" which dispersed the viruses also carried cameras to assist in observation, but small ground-cars were also made available to the observers. This group was headed by Gregor Zuvara, who had become an expert on the Underworld by virtue of having spent a few more days there than most of those called in to assist him.

As the miniature city grew, Zuvara was forced to make ever-more-plaintive complaints about the inadequacy of his labor force. As soon as the news concerning the attack on Germont's force and the several deaths among his personnel was made public, the number of volunteers for work in the Underworld fell rapidly.

Within a matter of days it became obvious both above and below that some form of conscription would have to become effective. The subjugation of the individuals in the society of the Euchronian Millennium to necessity, as defined by the Hegemony of the Movement, became absolute. The clock had been turned right back. For the second time, the Euchronian Movement demanded total loyalty in order that the world might be saved, not for the present generation, but for generations to come.

Almost everyone expected this mobilization of Euchronia's manpower to go quite smoothly. This, after all, was the principle on which the world had been made. It had worked once—it had to work again. But Zuvara found his recruits resentful and discontent. The Euchronian spirit—the determination and selflessness that had built a world on the roof of a ruined Earth—was lacking.

Slowly, Zuvara realized that everything had changed. The Euchronian ideal was not enough. Not this time. Something within society had shattered.

While he watched the blight he had brought spreading throughout the world, stripping the vast marshland of everything living, reducing all plant tissue to a sort of protoplasmic tar, Zuvara could not help thinking: "We are destroying the world. The whole world. We are doing this to *ourselves. Everything* will die. There will be nothing left."

He told himself over and over that this was merely a nightmare, but he could not rid himself of it.

9.

Chemec the cripple had left Shairn with Camlak because the way his mind worked left him little option but to follow his leader. Camlak had been Old Man of Stalhelm—virtually all that was left of Stalhelm. He had been all that was left of Chemec's life.

Now Camlak was gone, and there was virtually nothing left of Chemec's existence. Nothing but his cunning and his failing strength, and his meager identity: Chemec the crab, Chemec the bent-leg. But Chemec hardly felt a sense of loss. Certainly he did not grieve for Camlak. Chemec took life as it came, and accepted events as they happened. He lived neither in his memories nor in his hopes, but stayed always within the moment of the ephemeral present, carried along by the current of life. It was the way of his kind, and Chemec was very much one of his kind. More so than Camlak or Nita, or even Old Man Yami.

It was because of what he was rather than in spite of it that Chemec became a prophet. He had never been a man at odds with his soul. He coexisted with the Gray Soul inside his mind, in the simplest possible way. It was there, he let it be. He had never tried to be a psychic parasite with regard to his Gray Soul, nor had he attempted any kind of exchange. At Communion, he merely looked his Soul in the face. Nothing more. It was perfect commensalism—Chemec and the Soul shared the body and the mind, and neither troubled the other.

And because of this, when the Soul began placing motives in his mind, Chemec did not realize what was happening. He accepted the motives as his own, and he obeyed their commands as if they came from his own self.

He needed the motives. With Camlak gone, he had nothing left to him but to drift back into Shairn, to find a new community or to live alone, existing until he died. The motives made something of him. They repaired the aspect of function in his life. They made him a man again, whereas he might otherwise have contented himself as a rat.

From the Swithering Waste he went southwest, and came to the townships of northern Shairn: to Isthomi and Escar, to Rocoral and Zeid. In each town, he persuaded the priests to look into their soul-space, and he caused Communions to be called. At the Communions, he preached, and because of the Gray Souls his words were heard and engraved into the minds of his hearers.

All had heard Camlak's scream and knew intuitively that something of moment had happened at that moment. They were ready to hear—and so were the Gray Souls.

Chemec warned of the coming of the men from Heaven—of the impending destruction of the world. This was prophecy. He described things which he had seen, and things which were yet to be seen. What he said was true.

He did no more than this—his function was to spread the word, and no more. His function was to alert the Children of the Voice in Shairn. Others took his warnings beyond Shairn, into other parts of the world. While Chemec prepared for the uniting of a nation, others made way for the uniting of a race.

And in all parts of the world, while the warning was carried, the priesthood of the Children of the Voice, in rapport with their Gray Souls, attempted to decide and define what role the Children of the Voice were to play in the coming climax of their world.

10.

Everyone in Euchronia was familiar with the game called Hoh. It was played everywhere. Passionate believers in Euchronian ideology tended to be passionate Hoh players as well. Rafael Heres and Eliot Rypeck were both expert players. Perhaps strangely, some of the most dedicated opponents of political Euchronianism were also devoted to the game. Thorold Warnet was one. There was, however, a sharp difference between the kinds of strategy that the opposing groups favored.

If it could be said that there was a single key to Euchronian civilization—one social institution which could help one to understand the way that the Overworld society worked—then that key had to be Hoh.

All games are, to some extent, analogues of life situations. One can learn a great deal about relationships within a society from a study of the way popular games are staged and used by the members of the society, and from the kind of encounter mimicked by the rules of such games. The simplest games are redistribution-of-capital games, usually governed by sheer chance. Such games become complicated by the addition of player-options rather than by the introduction of manipulative skill. Other games which usually exist alongside these are war games, in which chance is minimized and skill becomes paramount. All games of this class are zero-sum games, in which one player's gain is another's loss. There are other kinds of games—accumulation or construction games—which are not zero-sum. In a society dominated by zero-sum concerns, this class is primarily represented by one-player games rather than group-competitive games.

The game of Hoh was a complex derivation of a much older game which consisted of locating dots on a matrix, and establishing rules determining conditions under which they "die," "survive," or "reproduce." As these rules are followed, the population of dots passes through a number of "generations" and—ultimately onc of several results is obtained. All the dots may be removed from the board; a pattern may form which reproduces itself exactly at each generation; a stable cycle of patterns may result; or a pattern may be formed which reproduces itself and simultaneously changes location so that it "migrates" across the matrix. This game is an elementary simulation of a population attempting to become viable. The rate of success or failure depends on two things: the rules governing death, survival and reproduction; and the initial pattern established on the matrix. Player participation is introduced if the player is permitted to "move" dots at each generation, according to options regulated by further rules. In its basic form, this is a one-player game. It becomes a multiple-player game when more than one population is introduced into the matrix, "competing" for available space. Again, new rules have to be introduced to govern interspecific interaction as well as infraspecific. All the original outcomes are preserved with respect to either population. Several different "target situations" are possible: players may attempt to stabilize their own population and exterminate all others, or the players may collaborate so that *all* the populations become stable and viable. If "winning" is defined as stabilizing the particular population under a player's control, then the game may have only one winner, or no winners at all, or all the players might win.

In Hoh, the factor of evolution is added to the competition situation, providing for populations to change their properties as defined by the rules. The ability to do so, like the ability of the population to redeploy itself at each generation, is controlled by player-options.

The Hoh player, therefore, has a number of options open to him strategically. He may direct his efforts toward the situation in which his population alone survives, or toward a situation in which more than one—perhaps all—the populations survive. In so doing, he may endeavor to alter the properties of his own pieces with respect to one another and to other pieces in order to make them more efficient at survival or reproduction, or "killing" pieces of other species. The rules are complex, and if the matrix on which the game is played is large, a computer is required to alter the pattern at each generation.

The Euchronian Movement was founded in order to stabilize the human population of Earth and to provide a social pattern for the resultant society. The Euchronian Movement, in effect, played a game analogous to Hoh in reality, and the Euchronian Plan by which a platform was built to cover the entire land surface of the planet, was a sequence of moves—a strategy—for such a game. The fact that a game like Hoh should have developed within Euchronian society to the preeminence which it eventually acquired was an eloquent testimony to the success of Euchronian ideology as a socially cohesive force. It was highly significant that political polarization in Euchronian society, during and after the completion of the Plan, should be correlated with different approaches to the game rather than with the evolution of alternative classes of game.

The dedicated Euchronians always played Hoh by strategies which would allow the maximum possible number of players to succeed in stabilization: they aimed toward the situation in which all populations became viable. This is not any easy way to play. Even if *all* the players work toward this end, the element of competition is not removed from the game, because it is built into the rules governing interactions. On a small matrix, it may be almost impossible to discover a situation in which four or five populations may collaborate in a stable situation, and even if one such situation exists, it may be impossible for any sequence of moves to bring that situation into being. In the eventuality of one or more players adopting a different strategy, the problems become complex indeed, as such players must be forced to conform, or be eliminated—problems of this type become inordinately complicated.

The Eupsychians who played Hoh almost invariably attempted to win outright—that is, to be the *only* winner. When Eupsychians played one another, the game was usually straightforward, and when Euchronians played together it was moderately so. The most interesting games, however, were played by Euchronians *and* Eupsychians. These games were the most difficult and the most challenging. Strangely, however, they took place rarely, even among the most expert players. Certainly Rafael Heres would never have sat down to play Hoh with anyone who was liable to employ Eupsychian strategies— not because he was afraid of the competition, but because he felt such strategies were contrary to the *spirit* in which the game ought to be played. Eupsychians used the same logic.

A Eupsychian would argue that Euchronians played toward an end that was "unnatural." They would cite the biological principle known as Gause's axiom, which states that two species in competition cannot coexist—one must always drive out or eliminate the other. The Euchronians worked toward an end that was perfectly possible and perfectly legitimate under the rules of Hoh, but the Eupsychian would nevertheless feel that they were "cheating" with respect to some more abstract principle.

A Euchronian, on the other hand, would argue that Eupsychian players were both narrow-minded and simple-minded, and deliberately unintelligent. He would point out that if the moves were made at random, then Gause's axiom would probably hold up in virtually every instance. *But*, he would say, the whole point of having intelligent, calculating players was to rise above the random situation: to control the game, and to force the situations which would not otherwise be probable. In nature, he would claim, Gause's axiom might have some validity, but when applied analogically to the game of Hoh, it ought to exist in order to be broken. Hoh was a game played with the aid of computers—it was the game of a highly advanced technological society—and it hardly made sense, to a Euchronian, that it should be played according to the law of the jungle.

It was, however, noticeable that when Euchronians and Eupsychians did sit down to participate mutually in a game of Hoh, the Euchronians—unless they were vastly superior players—could not reach the ideal target situation. At best, they could usually eliminate the Eupsychians by collective action in violation of their own principles, and then reorder their affairs to assure that they themselves were collaborative winners. In most instances, the Euchronians had to outnumber the Eupsychians considerably in order to stay in the game.

Significantly, an inordinately high percentage of games in which both Euchronians and Eupsychians participated, regardless of relative numbers, ended in the situation where no population was able to become viable. Normally, therefore, when Euchronians and Eupsychians played together, everybody lost.

11.

Yvon Emerich took pride in two things: his independence and his showmanship. Under normal circumstances, he had every opportunity to assert both these aspects of his character through his work in the holovisual media. Since the crisis, however, he had been removed utterly and totally from all assertive situations.

Formerly, he had been a kind of opposition that the Hegemony of the Euchronian Movement found advantageous to themselves. Emerich was anti-Council and anti-Heres, but he was also anti-everything else. He influenced opinion without controlling it in any way. He was a noncreative thinker, purely destructive in argument. He voiced perpetual objections to Council policy and behavior, but provided no alternatives. While he represented the voice of dissatisfaction, the Council was always secure, because there was never any pressure upon them to act differently, merely a perpetual challenge to justify the action which they took. Emerich gave resentment a focus, directing it away from channels where it might have become a threat to the power of the Movement. Though the society of the Euchronian Millennium was by no means the perfect world which had always been the Movement's promise, and though social unrest was evident in a hundred ways, the only real opposition to the Euchronian Movement—the Eupsychian party— had never gained a place on the Council in an election. Most people thought of Emerich as a Eupsychian, or at least a sympathizer, but he was by no means the kind of mouthpiece the party wanted or needed. From their point of view the association in the public mind was a handicap.

When the "invasion" of the Overworld had taken place, however, Emerich had become a luxury that the Council could no longer afford. They wanted no challenge to Heres' proposals— they did not even want it spoken aloud that the proposals (and the objectives) *could* be challenged. Heres wanted total control of the electronic media during the period of crisis, because after saving the world, he had to save Euchronia, and he knew full well that even if he succeeded in the former purpose, the latter might well be impossible. But in deposing Emerich from his position of preeminence he made himself a very determined enemy. From Emerich's point of view, necessity was no excuse for the injury and the insult which had been done to him.

The Eupsychians wasted no time whatsoever in taking advantage of this situation.

"The Movement," Thorold Warnet told him, "is finished. It's clinging to power now simply because there seems to be nothing to take its place. We must organize something to take its place. In order to do so, we need control of the cybernet, including communications."

"You want me to join the revolution?" said Emerich bluntly.

"Not quite," said Warnet. "We want you to stop the revolution—the revolution of the people against this crazy trap they find themselves in. At the moment, there's virtually nothing keeping the world running. Every citizen of Euchronia's Millennium is on the verge of insanity. Every one of us has been led to accept that Euchronia has absolute control. Education says so, and history says so. The Movement did the impossible, and built a new world out of the ruins of the old. We have all been taught that Euchronia is omnipotent, that society is stable and secure and completely ordered. That's all been wiped out in a single night. All it took was the revelation that something exists which Euchronia can't handle, can't control, can't bring under the aegis of its total order and stability. All that Euchronia can do is destroy—if it can even do that. But the destruction itself testifies to the redundancy of Euchronian belief. If Euchronia is omnipotent, it shouldn't have to react this way. The destruction of the Underworld may take care of the problem, but it's not an answer. There is no answer. The answer is for someone else to provide—not the Movement. We can provide one. What we need is someone to deliver it."

"Crap!" said Emerich. "As long as I can remember you people

have been spouting garbage like that. It means nothing. If you want to talk to me, talk sense. You want Heres out, fine. But don't tell me why—tell me *how.* What are you going to do, and what the hell makes you think it might *work?*"

Warnet felt like laughing at the short, plump man who contrived to know everything by refusing to admit anything. But Emerich was right. Exquisite analyses of the philosophical complexion of the situation, correct or not, were meaning-less. The important thing was to discover a program of action. Unfortunately, the argument between the Eupsychians and the Euchronian Movement had been so long confined to philosoph-ical argument that prescriptions for social action were not easy to come by.

"We know what we want to achieve," said Warnet. "The trouble is coordinating our efforts. We know how and where to act in order to take control out of Heres' hands into our own. What we don't have is a way of keeping control—of preventing complete chaos. It's no good taking the reins of government if the people react by becoming ungovernable. Somehow, we have to make them trust us. You're the only man in the world who can do that, because you're the only one who knows how. If you collaborate with us, I think it can be done—I think we can find a way. If not, then I think the entire structure of society may break down, and we'll have no government at all. In a world like ours, that would be total disaster. If a mechanized society doesn't function as a unit, then it will stop functioning alto-gether."

"All very fine," said Emerich. "But what about the Underworld?"

"Perhaps we can destroy it," said Warnet. "But we may have to come to terms with it. We're not committed. Heres is. That's all the difference there can be."

12.

When the last of the armored trucks had passed, the three came out of the forest and stood on the apron. The carpet of plants had been so badly cut and crushed by the tires that the ancient road surface was exposed here and there.

As the roar of the engines died away into the distance, the return of the silence seemed momentarily unnatural. The silence was real: nothing moved within the forest, no moths or birds called as they fluttered, even the whisper of the Overworld was still in this region.

"The road leads to Heaven," said Huldi, her eyes still fixed on the smear of light which marked the horizon where the trucks had gone.

"Perhaps," said Iorga.

Nita looked up, into the sky, to the roof of the world in which the stars were set. It seemed so very high above the world beneath. The dull gleam of the nearest pillars, set well back from the road yet still managing to catch a little of the starlight, seemed to stretch a long way. The pillars had always seemed to Nita to be as tall as anything could be, to set a limit to the tallness which anything could achieve. And yet the road *could* go to Heaven. Iorga had told her that he had seen mountains whose slopes went as far as the roof, and perhaps further. And in places the Overworld sagged, extending itself deep into the world beneath, at places like the metal wall. That the road went to Heaven even seemed to her to be some justification of the fact that it extended across hundreds of miles of blackland. It stood to reason that a road to Heaven would be a long road and a hard road, and one not easily followed. The blackland must be the borderland—the barrier-land—between the world which Shairn shared and the world from which Joth had come. That there was a road across the border, through the barrier, seemed to her to be significant. Everyone in Shairn knew of the road of stars, but no one, so far as she knew, was aware of where it went, or had ever attempted to follow it. It had been a challenge the Shaira had refused. But perhaps it was *for* the Shaira, so that those with the curiosity and the courage might be able to gain the sight of Heaven that her father had always wanted. Perhaps the road had been waiting for the Shaira—waiting since the beginning of time.

The alternative possibility—that the road existed not to permit the Shaira access to Heaven, but to permit the men of the Overworld access to Hell—did not occur to her. In her view, the men from the world above must have many ways of descending into the Tartarean realms. Logically, it was passage in the other way which would be difficult and hazardous.

They continued on their way, without speaking. They talked more between themselves now than they had previously, but they talked mostly when they rested to eat and sleep. They spoke about themselves, told things that they knew, and recalled images from the past. They did it without questions, because none of them was habituated to questions. But they all remembered Joth, who had been saturated with them. It was really his questions that they were answering, still.

They did not know how far they had come into the blackland, nor how far they might have to go before they reached some kind of a destination. But they kept on going, and they would continue for as long as it took to get to wherever they were going. There was never any temptation to give up and go back, because they were never conscious of the time that was being absorbed by the journey. As they were now, they were in passage, and they might have set out a moment before or a hundred years. The end of the journey might be just outside the blur which limited their sight, or they might be traveling forever, until they died. Such possibilities never came into their minds. Once they had accepted a purpose, they continued until the situation changed and events deflected them from their course.

The trek along the road of stars had not been without incident—several times (they had not bothered to count how many) they had been forced to defend themselves against slinking predators which had come too close. Some they had killed and eaten. But the predators were relatively few, and they were not the most serious danger. The real threat to the success of their journey was poison. In the blacklands, there was poison everywhere. The land which the Overworlders had left, in and about their cities, had been poisoned ten thousand years before, and as the Underworld life-system had become viable in these areas, as it had everywhere else, it had simply adapted to the poisons. Now, while the Overworld still pumped such wastes that it would not or could not reclaim down to the blackland surface, the life of the Underworld thrived on a constant supply of chemical and radioactive substance which would have been deadly to organisms elsewhere. The Underworld's life-system was by no means homogeneous. The Overworld had provided itself with a stable biotic environment as well as a mechanical and sociocultural one, but the Underworld could not and had not. Adaptation had required adaptation to a vast range of habitats. Perhaps the blacklands posed less of a threat to the people of the Underworld than to the Overworlders, but its dangers were nonetheless considerable. There was food here that they could eat, and water to be found that they could drink, but it was not easy to find or identify sources of their needs. And the worst of the trouble was that if they were selective, the parasites were not. A hundred or a thousand kinds of worm and winged thing would find them perfect hosts, while they would find the parasites deadly companions simply because of the poisons to which the tiny creatures were so adapted that they carried them around inside them in concentrations which Iorga, Nita and Huldi would find fatally toxic.

Even in the Swithering Waste, which was a wilderness, but a wilderness of the lightlands, Iorga had failed in a long fight against parasites and lost his mate. Here, the danger was exaggerated and ever-present. That was the true hazard of the blacklands, and that was why no one came here by choice, except perhaps the Cuchumanates, who had used the road for so long that they were probably made of poison themselves.

A little further along the way, they found one of the Cuchumanates, where rocks had spilled out over the road. One of the trucks had run right over her, and her body was smashed.

One of the trucks also remained. It had been caught broadside by the full force of the slippage, and had been turned on its side and carried off the road to smack into the slope on the far side, ending up sandwiched between two faces of rock and soil. The tires had not burst, but the suspension of the wheels had been so badly twisted that there had been no possible hope of getting the vehicle going even had the men from Heaven been able to dig it out. The truck had been resealed at the back, and it had obviously defied the attempts of the Cuchumanates to break into it after the convoy had gone. There were scars where the locking mechanism had been attacked with rocks, but it had not yielded.

Iorga made a brief attempt to do what the Cuchumanates had been unable to do, but it was only a token gesture. The vehicle was built too solidly for his meager resources.

The proximity of the Cuchumanates—there might be ten or a dozen in the group—was an extra reason for alertness. The species was quite unpredictable, and there was every reason to suppose that having lost at least one of their number recently the group would be ready enough to attack anyone or anything they met. Their weapons would undoubtedly be inferior—Iorga still had a gun—but that would not necessarily be significant in determining the outcome of a pitched battle.

They had no option but to move on quickly to a place where the road was clear, and not so confined by the looming forest. They walked for many miles before they stopped once more to sleep.

13.

Abram Ravelvent came to see Joth face to face, rather than using the cybernet, because he felt an intense personal involvement in the affairs of Joth's family. He had never met Joth, but had been caught up inextricably in the tangled web of associations which surrounded him. It was Ravelvent who had found for Carl Magner a staircase into the Underworld, and had taken him there, and had seen Simkin Cinner shoot Magner dead. Ravelvent had returned to that same spot, on a different occasion, to find Julea Magner waiting there—waiting for nothing.

Ravelvent half-hated Joth for what had been done to Julea, but reason would not let him blame the youth. He did not find Joth's metal face frightening or intimidating. He found it, if anything, more comfortable to face than most faces of flesh. It was a machine, and Ravelvent found the machineness of it easy to deal with. To Ravelvent, all faces were properties of a machine—the cybernet—and they were only difficult to understand when they pretended to be real: flesh and blood instead of image.

Ravelvent had never married, and had never lived with a woman until he took Julea Magner into his home following her abandonment outside the plexus.

"How is she?" asked Joth.

"Hurt."

"Why didn't she come? I tried to call, but the house was empty, and the net couldn't locate her. You must have done that."

"She thinks you're dead," said Ravelvent.

"Why?"

"You shouldn't have taken her with you. Why did you let her see what happened at Harkanter's house?"

"I didn't know it was going to happen."

"You let her see the one in the cage. And the other one—the cat-man."

"I let her see them," agreed Joth. "I wanted her to see them. I'd have liked the whole world to see them, not as they wanted to see them, but as they are. But the world won't believe in them. It believes in cats and rats and monsters instead. Is that what *she* believes too? That's not what I showed her. I showed her men."

"You left her in the car when you went back down."

"Should I have taken her with me?"

"You shouldn't have gone down. You should have stayed."

"I couldn't."

Ravelvent shook his head. "You don't realize what has happened to her. Her whole world has just been screwed up and thrown away. Everything she knew, everything she loved, everything that meant anything to her. It all dissolved, and left nothing but chaos. Ryan went into the Underworld, and never came back. Her father was shot in front of her, and he expended his dying breaths running down a staircase—into the Underworld. She sent you after Ryan, and she thought that you were dead, too. But you came back. You gave her some kind of hope. And what then? You brought the Underworld into her world along with you, and then you went back. You left her in the car and you went back. What had she left? Had she even some vestige of hope? I found her there, and she couldn't even talk to me. She could speak, and make words, but she had nothing to say. Once she'd told me what happened—some of it—she had no more to say. There's nothing left of her life, except the dreams which killed her father. You even brought her those."

"It wasn't my fault," said Joth, quietly.

"No? None of it?"

"I'm sorry," said Joth. "You have no idea how sorry I am. She's my sister. She didn't want any part of this—she was caught up in it, because she was Carl Magner's daughter, just as I was caught up in it because I am his son. And the whole world is caught up in it because it was Carl Magner's world. She was hurt, and I'm bitterly sorry that she's hurt. She's lost her world, you say. It's just been ripped away from her. But remember how easily the world tore, how simple it was to crumple it up and throw it away. Whose fault is that? Nobody's to blame. All that happened is that we discovered that the Underworld still exists, that the Euchronian Heaven isn't ten thousand years away from the Hell it ran away from. That's all. Julea was too close to that discovery. So was I. So were you. But there's no point in looking around for someone to blame, whether it's me or my father or Heres or the Children of the Voice or the founder of the Movement of God Almighty. What we have to do is put it *right*."

Ravelvent did not speak for several minutes. When he did, he said: "Why should *she* have to suffer?"

"I'm sorry," said Joth, again. "I'm sorry I had to use her to get into Harkanter's house. But what else could I do? Would he have opened the door to me? To Iorga? I was trying to put things right. It wasn't my fault that everything blew up in my face. I'm still trying to put things right. I'm trying to stop them destroying the Underworld. But they don't listen. They just won't *see*."

"They *can't*," said Ravelvent. "You must understand that."

"I don't. I don't understand it at all."

"You've been into the Underworld," Said Ravelvent. "You've lived there. I don't know how, but somehow it's become real to you. It's not real to me. I *know* it's real, intellectually. I can consider it as a fact, I can think about it with complete rationality. People ask me questions, and I can give them answers. I can offer opinions, make predictions, analyze and theorize. But I can't make it real.

"I'm an old man, Joth. Most of us are old, because we can live a long time, and our birth rate isn't large. Maybe that's what makes the difference. The Underworld, to me, is just not real. It's a fantasy. There just is no place in my mind which can accept the reality of the things which you have revealed—or even the things which are happening in the world. Until the last few days I never had a bad dream in my life. Now all my dreams are nightmares. Even while I'm awake, things come into my mind that make me think I'm mad. I don't accept the reality of these things, because there's no way I can. To me, it seems that the world is becoming *unreal*.

"You don't understand why people can't accept what you tell them. I don't understand it either, but I know that it's so. The things which you talk about are beyond our conceptual horizons. It was the same with your father's book. Many of us found it fascinating, but in a purely speculative sense. It wouldn't have mattered if everything your father wrote had been true, and demonstrably true, because we simply aren't mentally constructed in order to accept it as true. We can talk about the Underworld, and appear to do so quite sensibly, but it's as though we were trying to solve a puzzle. What's worse is the fact that we know we're wrong—we know that we're failing to confront the problem, not even beginning to come to terms with it. And we're *frightened*. But our minds just aren't equipped to face up to what's happening. If it goes on, we'll *all* end up like Julea. Our worlds will simply dissolve."

For the first time, Joth realized how badly Ravelvent was disturbed. And not just Ravelvent. Rypeck and Ulicon too. Perhaps everyone who had been affected by Camlak's mind-blast. He began to understand why he seemed to be on a totally different wavelength whenever he talked to Rypeck of Ulicon. He discovered a new dimension to the problem. This, he thought, is why they seem to struggle so desperately to understand, and yet never gain any real insight. Ravelvent's phrase *"beyond our conceptual horizons"* echoed in his mind.

"If that's so," he whispered, more to himself than to Ravelvent, *"what makes me different?"*

14.

As Rypeck looked at Heres' image in the screen, he could almost sense the mental blockade which the Hegemon had built. The hostility and rancor which existed between them had supposedly been left behind when the crisis arose, but its legacy was still there. And there was more. It was not simply that Heres did not want to listen to Rypeck. Heres did not want to listen at all. He no longer wanted to hear anything. He had already made up his mind. He was entrenched so deeply and so firmly that no other assault upon his sense of reality could possibly succeed.

Perhaps he was insane. Or perhaps it was the world which was insane.

This time, though, it didn't seem to matter to Rypeck. He no longer wanted to steer Heres away from one course to another. It wouldn't really matter at all whether Heres listened to him or not.

"It's too late," he said. "We've already lost."

"If we can muster the powers at our disposal," said Heres definitely, "then we will be safe. All that we require is the level of commitment that our forefathers gave to the Euchronian Plan. If we can all come together and give our utmost to the project, then we must succeed. We will not fail."

"That speech is eleven thousand years out of date," said Rypeck. "And so are we."

"You're supposed to be reporting to me on what you found out from Joth Magner," said Heres. "Every time you speak to me you begin like this, with deliberately veiled comments which you hurl at me as if you were throwing stones. It's only your way, I know, but it's tiresome. What have you found out?"

"There are at least three, and probably more, intelligent species in the Underworld. There are humans, and animals which have evolved to mimic humans—rats and cats. All these races share cultural as well as biological similarities. There appears to be no genetic intercourse between the races—that's almost certainly impossible, because they aren't related enough to hybridize—but there's a good deal of intellectual intercourse. Ideas don't obey the principles of heredity, and cultural evolution isn't subject to Darwinian selection. So both the cats and the rats have absorbed human culture and habits, once having evolved physically to the point where their brains could take it. It is, therefore, just as meaningful to call Harkanter's specimen a man as it is to call it a rat. That's the first thing you should know.

"Secondly, we have every reason to believe that the mental blast, or invasion, or whatever you want to call it, was not a deliberate act in itself, but the side effect of whatever the rat did to remove itself from that cage. We suggest that what happened was that the rat wanted to escape from its predicament, and it twisted itself into another space parallel to our own. The energy of the translocation manifested itself in the way we experienced.

"There are several million of these creatures in the Underworld. It is possible that every single one is capable of doing what Harkanter's specimen did. If you attempt to destroy them, they might very probably do so. On the other hand, if we do nothing, it seems likely that it will happen again anyway. Even if it doesn't, the evidence is that many people have been sensitized by the experience, and are now in the same situation as Magner—while they sleep their minds can pick up images carried by energy waves of this type radiating from the Underworld—presumably from the brains of the rats.

"So, as I said, it's too late. It doesn't matter what you decide to do. Not anymore. We're on borrowed time, Rafe."

"If what you say is true," said Heres, "then we must destroy these rats completely."

"I doubt whether you can," said Rypeck. "They received the broadcast from the rat's mind just as we did—except that they're in a much better position to make sense of it. They know the trick can be done, and they almost certainly know how to do it now, even if they didn't before."

"There has been no repetition."

"Not yet."

"So we must act quickly. Germont's force will move into the lighted area very soon now, and we should also have reports on the effect of the seeding by tonight. It will take some time to achieve the levels of production which we need, even if the seeding experiments are totally successful, but it can be done."

"All we have to do is keep mind and body together," said Rypeck drily.

"If we remain calm and self-disciplined," said Heres, "there should be no difficulty."

"You're wrong, Rafe. You're dead wrong. Our minds just can't stand up to any of this. We should have guessed earlier. Our fathers and our grandfathers shpuld have guessed. But they only saw the useful aspects of i-minus. For thousands of years now, the i-minus agent has been censoring our dreams, tidying up our minds, making us utterly and completely children of the Euchronian way of life. Maybe i-minus saved the Plan, by shaping the workers so carefully to their purpose in life. But i-minus has made us all into mental cripples. It has bound us so closely to Euchronia that we are no longer capable of looking beyond Euchronia. We have adapted ourselves too closely, in mind rather than in body, to the Overworld. We've become parasites within the cybercomplex, and parasites always evolve to become totally dependent—they lose their adaptability. That's what's happened to us, Rafe. We have no mental adaptability. None whatsoever. We believed so utterly and completely in Euchronia and in nothing else that our minds were simply ready to shatter at the discovery of anything new.

"The disaster has already happened, and there's no way back. You can try to destroy the universe, Rafe, if you want to. But you can't remain calm and undisciplined. You can't face up to the situation. It's the simplest little things that are beyond you, even though you rule the world."

"Eliot," said Heres, "I think that you're cracking up. I think you may be going mad."

"I think you're right," said Rypeck. "For more than a hundred years, I knew nothing but Heaven. Now I have looked into Hell. How can the sanity I had then help me now? Carl Magner wrote a book about *The Marriage of Heaven and Hell*. That marriage has taken place, in my mind as in yours. There can't be any divorce. Not ever."

Heres never heard the end of that particular speech. He had switched off the cyberlink halfway through.

15.

Gregor Zuvara and Felipe Rath, with half a dozen others, were in the largest of the plastic domes in their Underworld city. More than any of the others, this was obviously an extension of the mechanical organism which covered the continents of the world. It was packed with equipment as sophisticated as any in the upper world, and all of the electronic devices were in constant communication with the cybernet and all its facilities. Once inside the dome it was quite easy to imagine that one was on the platform rather than the surface. The only thing which testified clearly to the fact that these men were on an alien and hostile world was the fact that they were physically together, sharing the same space and the same air.

Vicente Soron entered through the complex doors, disrobing and submitting to sterilization procedure with angry impatience. As soon as those inside saw him it was obvious to them that something was very wrong.

He went to Zuvara and said: "We have to talk in private."

"Why?"

This question came from Rath, not from Zuvara. Soron looked around, and saw that every eye was upon him, and that every ear was listening. He licked his lips.

"It's important," he said.

"If it's important," said Rath, cutting in just as Zuvara was about to reply, "then I want to hear it. We all want to hear it." His voice was strained, and he seemed to be on edge.

"I think you'd better tell us all," said Zuvara, in a low voice.

Soron looked at Rath, then at Zuvara, and it struck him very suddenly and very strongly that they already knew what he had to say. Something had frightened them, and frightened them badly. The news which he had to impart had been thrusting at his throat, the words waiting to tumble out just as soon as he could get Zuvara alone. But his need to talk died away suddenly.

"What's the matter?" he asked.

"You tell us," said Rath.

Zuvara waved at him impatiently, trying to shut him up. "Something's wrong, Vicente. If that's what you've come to tell us, don't bother. We've lost contact with Germont's Delta contingent. We think that they're all dead."

For a few seconds, what Zuvara had said simply did not make

sense to Soron. He repeated the words over in his mind, but still they evaded him. Then he realized what he had been told. They didn't know at all. This was different—something entirely unexpected.

"What happened?" he asked.

"We don't know," said Rath, again quick to interrupt. "We got no message. Nothing. Whatever it was must have killed them quickly, and without any warning. Now, if there's anything we should know, you'd better tell us, because if the same thing is going to happen to us, we want warning."

Soron shook his head slowly. "No," he said. "It's something entirely different."

"It's throwing quite some panic into you," observed, Rath.

"I can't tell you," said Soron. "The Council has to know. It's for them to decide what's to be done. I daren't release the information to anyone except Gregor. Not until the Council knows."

"You'd better...," Zuvara began, but again Rath was ahead of him. Rath was almost shaking, and his face was white. Soron realized that the news about the lost vehicles must only just have come in. It must have had a profound effect upon the men in the encampment, who had been in the Underworld for some time now, and were beginning to hate every moment of it as it became obvious that the likelihood of an early return to the Overworld was out of the question. Rath, Zuvara and Soron had all come down with Harkanter's party—to look around, to see what the Underworld was like. It had been a game then. Now, it was no longer a game. Cut off from the world they knew, with the mechanical extensions of the cybernet more an accentuation of their removal than an amelioration of it, they had begun to sense imminent danger everywhere in the dead, decaying land that surrounded the dome city.

"The Council," said Rath, "are up there. We're here. Never mind relaying information to the Council so that they can alert us at their pleasure. We should be the first to know, not the last."

"This shouldn't be made public," insisted Soron.

"Let's *all* be the judge of that," said Rath. "We want to know.

Are the plants withstanding the seeding? Don't the diseases work as well as they should? Is there an army marching from the south? What's wrong, man?" Soron wiped his mouth, and turned away for a moment. Zuvara said nothing, now that he had the opportunity. He waited, with Rath and the others.

"I've been out in the southeast sector," he said. "Checking the progress of the viruses. Everything seems to be dying, all right. Everywhere is covered in gray slime. Literally everywhere. Including the pillars which support the platform. You know how they have lichens and small prokaryot cells growing all over them. The encrustation on every pillar is dying, and you can just scrape the stuff away. That's what I did.

"Some of it must have been chemosynthetic. Some of the stuff has eaten its way back into the pillars half an inch or more. The surface under the crust is corroded and pitted."

He stopped and waited, but no one said a word.

"Don't you see?" he said. "The columns which support the Overworld are being steadily weakened. And we knew nothing about it. Sections of the platform may already be in danger. It may begin to collapse at any time. Tomorrow, or next year. We simply don't know."

16.

"I come to you," said Heres, "as my ancestors came to you some thousands of years ago. I need your help. The world which you helped to build—your world—needs your help."

Sisyr's expression did not change, but he seemed suddenly very thoughtful. The alien was considerably taller than the Hegemon, but they were both seated, and the difference was not obvious. They were dressed in the same type of clothing.

But the alien's skin was red-brown. His eyes were round, and had no pupils, being uniformly pale blue in color. A darker area of soft tissue served as both nasal organ and upper lip. The lower jaw closed behind this flap of tissue. Nevertheless, the face gave the impression of being "mammalian." It was not horrifying. The hands were different. There was something about the hands which suggested insects. Their structure was complex—far more so than human hands. The hard, thin fingers looked as if they might snap like pencils if pressure were applied to them.

It struck Heres most forcefully that there was a certain *hardness* about Sisyr's whole frame and bearing. He looked strong, not simply because of his height, but because of the way he held himself. Heres, for some reason, always saw human beings as *soft* creatures. The sensation of wearing his own skin always exaggerated in his mind the delicacy and vulnerability of flesh. Heres hated to scratch himself, and he was hypersensitive to pain.

"How can I help you?" asked Sisyr.

"Exactly as you did before," Heres replied. "You will advise us, and give us the benefit of your scientific knowledge and technical skill."

"Toward what end?" asked the alien.

Heres pursed his lips slightly. The alien knew perfectly well what end Heres had in mind. Why was he asking for it to be spelled out?

"Ultimately," said the Hegemon, "the security of the people of the Overworld. We wish to exterminate all sources of danger or potential danger on the planet."

"You want to extirpate life in the Underworld," stated Sisyr.

"It may be necessary," said Heres, smoothly. "We may be able to save many species of potential usefulness and harmlessness. If, with your help, we can weed out the inimical varieties, we may have the means to begin the work of remaking the surface of the Earth into a habitable environment. I have not abandoned that possibility."

"The Underworld is habitable now," said Sisyr.

"By habitable," Heres said, his voice still smooth and his manner unruffled, "I mean suitable for habitation by the standards of the Overworld."

"What you want me to do," said the alien, "is—as I understand it—help you to wage a war of extermination against the people of the Underworld."

"We need not consider them people," said the Hegemon. "'Even those of apparent human ancestry are now a genetically isolated species. They are not men, as we are men. They are evolutionary side branches. We are engaged in a struggle for existence. We cannot afford to handicap ourselves with philosophical niceties." While he delivered this speech, Heres recalled the very different ideas he had advanced while proclaiming to the world his Second Euchronian Plan for the reclamation of the Underworld. But circumstances had changed since then, and ideas had to be brought into line with circumstance.

"Why do you think that the Planners put lights in the Underworld?" asked Sisyr.

"Because they needed them," said Heres, "in the days when the platform was under construction, and there was constant intercourse between the two worlds."

"But the lights still burn."

"For now," said Heres, matching words unsaid with words unsaid.

"You know that I have been sending small quantities of material from the Overworld into the Underworld for thousands of years?" asked the alien. Without waiting for an answer, he continued: "Manufactured goods—mostly tools and books. All in the name of the Plan."

"It has been brought to my attention," said Heres.

"Do you know why?"

"If you say that it was provided for in the Plan," said the Hegemon, "then I cannot contradict you. But now the Plan has been changed. It is no longer required that you should distribute necessary materials in the Underworld, helping to keep its people alive and—to some degree—civilized. We have new priorities now."

Sisyr shook his head deliberately. The calm mimicry of the human gesture alarmed Heres. This creature had perfected a false humanity which existed alongside his real self. Heres, as a human, could confront only the human analogue, never the alien. There was no way to guess what Sisyr's priorities might be—what he thought and felt. There was no way to answer questions relating to the alien, like *why?* And *who?* As Heres watched the red-brown face, he tried to call to his own mind some appreciation of the fact that Sisyr was thousands of years old. He had lived on Earth for nearly ten thousand, and he might have been thousands, or millions of years old before his ship first came to Earth. Was he any nearer to death now? So far as Heres, or anyone else, was aware, the alien might outlast the Earth itself, and the sun, and the galaxy.

But Heres had no sense of the infinite. He could not begin to conceive of a span of time so vast that the things which Heres concerned himself with might be so evanescent as to be meaningless. And yet the alien lived second by second, hour by hour, just as Heres did. His past and his future might be infinitely extended, but his present moved at exactly the same pace from one to the other. Heres' affairs of the moment were Sisyr's too. And Sisyr had not been content to stand aside from the problem of the first Planners. He had involved himself. He had tried to become a part of Earth. He had made Earth his world.

"I cannot help you," said Sisyr.

Although he had expected this, Heres recoiled from the flat statement as if it were a physical blow.

"You must," he said....

Sisyr shook his head again.

"We have the power to compel you," said Heres. "You are subject to our laws."

"I have the right to refuse," said Sisyr. "I have the right to remain silent. You may pass judgment upon me, and I must accept the judgment. But you cannot compel me to do what I will not do."

Heres suppressed his anger with the ease of long practice. The anger was not insistent. It died at his command.

"Tell me why," he demanded.

"You know why," said the alien.

"You have a duty to us," said the Hegemon. "You helped us create this society. You have a responsibility toward it. You cannot stand by and see it destroyed. It is your fault that we are in such extreme danger now. Had you not continued to supply the Underworld, had you not provided them with light, they would not have survived. There would be no people of the Underworld. I am not accusing you or blaming you, I am simply stating the facts. No one will hold this against you. But the fact remains that you are responsible for the threat to the world which you helped to create. You cannot simply turn your back and deny involvement. You must take action now, along with the citizens of the Euchronian Millennium, to set aside the earlier actions which have led to this crisis. We demand your assistance. Without your knowledge we may very well fail to overcome the threat to our existence. But with your help we will be able to do what we have to as quickly and as cleanly as possible."

"I do not deny involvement," said Sisyr. "But I do deny commitment of the kind which you are trying to thrust upon me.

"I did not design and build the Overworld. That was the work of your Planners. What I did was to put within their reach the means by which they could bring their Plan into effect. I showed them how the platform could become an engineering possibility. I showed them how to make the best use of their raw materials. I showed them how to get the necessary power. But I did not create the Overworld. The world which *I* created was the Underworld.

"Your Planners were convinced that the surface was irrevocably ruined. They mistook the end of the environment to which they were adapted for the end of life, for the end of the world. They committed themselves entirely to the new world built above the old. That was their only hope—not for mankind, but for their particular image of man, for their particular human ambitions.

"I did for them what they wanted me to do. But at the same

time, I took what steps I could to assure the future of the Underworld. Life there would have survived in any case, without any intervention on my part. What would have happened there if I had not done as I did is not very different from what *has* happened there. Rapid divergent evolution of those forms best equipped to survive would have brought into being much the kind of life-system which has established itself. What I did was to contribute just a little to epiphenomenal continuity. I made certain things happen more quickly. Where chance might have resulted in two or several outcomes I made sure of one particular outcome.

"Your Planners wanted to save the human race which existed in their own imagination. I wanted to save several human races—several potential routes for human evolution. You say that the people of the Underworld need not be considered as people. They might say the same of you. Neither your human race nor any of theirs is the same human race which existed in prehistoric times. Nor was that race static in an evolutionary sense. Indeed, the human race readapted itself throughout its history with remarkable speed. Humanity has always practiced self-change. And it has always been able to pass on this self-change, not by heredity, but by control of the environments which shape the individual.

"Your Euchronians always believed that the process of self-change was directional, and that there was an end-point to it all. I helped them reach that particular end-point. You have found, of course, that there is no such end. Time does not stop. Change does not stop. If you wipe out all life on Earth except yourselves, and make the environment totally unchangeable, and—with the aid of your i-minus drugs—shape every member of your society as completely as possible to the Euchronian ideal, you will still find that there is no end. That is what I believe. I would not be alive if I did not.

"You cannot destroy the Underworld. If you kill every living thing within it, it will return, in time. And even in the meantime it will not be lost, because it exists inside you all, as a potential, as an alternative. In the same way, the Underworld cannot destroy you, even if it kills you all. Euchronia exists, if only as a possibility. No matter who, or where, or what you are, there are always Heaven and Hell. You cannot divide infinity and eternity. Wherever you draw a line, there is always infinity and eternity to either side of it."

"I'm not concerned with infinity and eternity," said Heres. "I'm only concerned with now."

"The identity you have shaped for yourself may not recognize its concern with infinity and eternity," said the alien, "but it is nevertheless contained therein. I *am* concerned with infinity and eternity, because I am eternal, and have access to infinity."

"If this is the way you think," said Heres, "then why did you help us in the first place?"

"Because I am concerned with preserving real alternatives," said the alien. "I am concerned with eternity, but I am also concerned with now. The present is where the eternal happens. Everything may come to one who waits, but he need not wait. He may act, and thus control what comes.

"You say I have a duty to my world—a duty to save it from destruction. That is what I intend to do. But my world is Earth, not Euchronia. I cannot help you."

"Then I must place you under arrest," said Heres. "According to the law, you are guilty of treason. And I warn you that we may be forced to discover ways by which we can make you help us."

Sisyr stared the Hegemon in the face, and he seemed for a moment to be preternaturally still.

"I doubt it," he said, quietly. "I doubt it."

17.

The three remaining contingents of Germont's force split up in the lightlands, and separated by some twenty or thirty miles, moving southeast into Shairn. Germont's own third of the force moved slightly ahead of the others, and it was this fraction which first came within sight of one of the villages of the Children of the Voice.

The column halted, and Germont asked for instructions from above.

The man to whom Germont was actually talking was Luel Dascon, who stood, in the present situation, second only to Heres. He was the only man whose loyalty Heres dared trust completely. Dascon could see what the village and its surrounds looked like by means of a camera eye mounted on Germont's vehicle.

What he saw was a wall of Earth, with the tops of tall conical roofs visible behind it. The land around the village had been divided up into rough squares thirty to a hundred yards in length, which were separated by footworn pathways. In these fields grew an assortment of plants, the most common of which was a dark gray thickset stalk with a paler bulb, rather like a foot-thick matchstick. In some of the fields compounds were divided out by walls of sod daubed with some white substance—apparently to stiffen the barriers. Within these compounds were animals: burly, pallid pigs.

There was no one working in the fields—in fact, there was no one visible outside the wall. A warning of the approach of the armored cars had been given some time previously, and the villagers had withdrawn. A few scattered heads were just visible at the wall.

A rough road—or, at least, a track rather wider than the footpaths in the fields—led away to the east, but it was impossible to follow its course across the terrain for more than a quarter of a mile.

"Move forward slowly," said Dascon. "Pass the village on the west side, staying well clear of the walls. Try to follow the paths through the fields, and spray the crop with the virus as you pass. Don't open fire on the village or the villagers unless they come out to attack. Ignore anything they throw or shoot from the wall."

"We could raze the village in under an hour," said Germont.

"That's the last thing we want at the moment," said Dascon. "There's a whole nation to the south of you. We don't want open war. We just want to destroy their food supply, quietly and completely. No matter how superior your firepower, pitched battles mean losses. You already know that."

"I'd be happier with them dead," Germont replied. He was convinced—although there was no evidence—that the contingent left behind in the blacklands had been destroyed by some mysterious mindpower of which the Underworlders were possessed. He was very frightened by the idea of such an insidious threat. Dascon, too, was anxious about the potential power of the Children of the Voice, but his approach to the problem was different. Fear made Germont want to shoot, and keep shooting—to eject the fear with the bullets, to be conscious that he was fighting back, was killing. Dascon was concerned that the rats should not be frightened, that they should be convinced that they had nothing to fear from the Overworld invasion, and would therefore fail to make use of the extraordinary action to which Camlak had been driven. Heres had decided that they should work on the theory that the Children of the Voice would accept the blight of all plant life in their area as a natural occurrence—merely an extension of disasters which must have happened before—and that they would not thereby be prompted into any unusual action.

The column moved forward slowly. Germont's driver took what seemed to the commander to be elaborate detours in order not to cut across any of the fields, destroying the standing crops. Some of the matchstick plants inevitably got crushed by the great wheels, but the damage was done in a tidy, orderly fashion.

The man at the machine gun was visibly nervous. He was above Germont's station, and his feet were not far away from Germont's face. The smell seemed very noticeable.

When they were closest to the village wall they were broadside-on, and the camera eye showed only empty land ahead. Germont moved to where he could see out of the cockpit, and relayed his impressions to Dascon.

"There are thirty or forty of them watching us over the wall," he said. "They seem patient and relaxed. I don't understand why there are no signs of fear or hostility. Trucks don't drive through their agricultural holdings every day—these things can never have seen a vehicle like this in their lives. They can't have got beyond the wheelbarrow themselves, without horses or cattle. I can't make out their eyes at this distance, and I presume the expressions on their faces wouldn't mean much to me anyhow, but the way they stand and watch suggests to me that they know—or think they know—exactly what we are and what we're doing. But they're making no move to stop us. It doesn't make sense to me."

"You're imagining things," Dascon told him. "They're probably scared to death."

"No," said Germont. "That's just not so." After a pause, he continued: "There's another gate on the south side, much larger than the ones to north and east. There's a road—a track of sorts—leading away south. Geographically, that should be the main road. The big gate is white, and looks for all the world to me as if it's made out of bones. Maybe that's so."

"Not necessarily sinister," said Dascon. "There's a shortage of woody tissue in the Underworld. They probably can't afford to waste bones—they have to use them for tools and frames. The supply of animal bones probably isn't enough."

"I don't care why they use bones," said Germont. "The fact that they do is enough for me. Mine are longer, and maybe tougher than theirs. They aren't going to lose any opportunities to kill us, once they're convinced they have a chance."

"You're safe enough," said Dascon drily.

"That's easy for you to say."

The column passed by the village without the slightest incident. Not a rock was thrown, nor a spear, nor an arrow loosed.

"I wish they'd come at us," said Germont. "I really do. That, I can understand. I can understand them coming out and attacking, and getting themselves shot to bits. I can understand them running or hiding. But the way they look says to me that they know something we don't. They have something all ready. It just looks to me as if they know we can't hurt them. I feel like a rat in a trap."

"Don't be a fool," said Dascon.

"Don't call me names," Germont snapped back. "If you want to pour scorn, you come down here and pour it. This is no picnic, Luel, and you know it. We've already lost more than a quarter of the force, and for what? Nothing. We don't even know how they died. We wouldn't know what killed them if it was inside with us now.

"And I'll tell you something else. When I look at the map and see what kind of distance we've covered these last few days, and what kind of area we *might* be infecting with these damned virus sprays, I begin to see how little impression we've made on this world. I tell you now that I'm not going to be here for years, and I don't think any of the men along with me are going to take it for much longer either."

"You won't need to be there much longer," said Dascon, soothingly. "Certainly not years. We don't need you to spread the virus—we need you to tell us what happens. You're observers. Once we know what to expect of the sprays, the seeding will be handled mechanically. Yours is just the test project. That's all. If you keep your eyes open, you won't die. Nothing can get at you inside the vehicles. Nothing at all. We'll know what happened to the Delta group in a matter of hours. Whatever mistake they made won't be repeated."

Germont found the calm voice extremely irritating. He had never liked Dascon. He *knew*, somewhere inside him, that Dascon was wrong. He was half-convinced that the team sent out to find out why the Delta contingent had disappeared or died would meet exactly the same fate, but he dared not make such a prediction out loud, in case it should be accurate.

He knew, also, by the same mysterious means, that the Children of the Voice could read his mind, and therefore anticipate his actions. It was the only explanation that made sense to him of the fact that the Underworlders were obviously not frightened of him.

He felt—to use the words of his own ironic simile—like a rat in a trap.

18.

There was a single searchlight burning, its beam pointing diagonally upward, like a finger of light. Near to the ground the beam was clear-cut, sharply defined by virtue of the dust that floated in the air. Higher up, it became dissipated, and ultimately lost. The roof of the world was too far away for a circle of reflected light to show upon its dark face.

Iorga knew when he was still a good distance away that the men from Heaven were all dead. There was no sound at all—no clink of metal against metal. Nothing moved in or around the vehicles. Such stillness could only mean death.

There had been a dozen vehicles in the Delta contingent of Jacob Germont's invasion force. They were huddled together in two lines of six, nose to tail. All the lights were dead except for the one lonely beam.

"Stay here," said Iorga. "Something bad. Something evil."

Nita looked around, at the bones of the city, beslimed with what had once been the forest, now decaying and putrefying. She shivered. She had never before been in the presence of such death—such all-consuming blight. She assumed that the death of the Heaven-sent was part and parcel of the death of the forest, and she could find no rationality in it, no meaning.

While Iorga went forward, Huldi and Nita hung back, crouching close together in the star-shadow of a crumbling wall.

The hellkin moved slowly, with the gun in his hands. He had faith in the gun, which had come from Heaven and must therefore be an answer to all possible perils, but he was cautious nevertheless. He did not want to use the weapon.

As he came closer, he saw that the vehicles were no longer

tightly sealed. The plastic windows in the front and in the side were gone—removed quite cleanly and totally. Then he noticed the tires. He recalled the truck which had been rendered useless by the landslip. It had had six wheels, all bearing massive black tires—gigantic things, four feet in diameter. The tires of these trucks had lost both shape and size—they had been partially dissolved and were still in the process of being dissolved. On the surface of the plastic mess was a thin silver sheen. Patches of the sheen were on the road, and on the blighted plant tissue which still decked the roadside structures.

When he came closer still, he could see that the interior of the lead vehicles was also covered with the thin slime. In the back of the cockpit of one of them there had been a man attending a gun. He was now a skeleton, but a skeleton which shone, glittering with soft reflected light, perhaps even giving out some light of its own: a bioluminescent glow.

They could not have noticed the invasion. It had come upon them while they rested, perhaps while most of them slept. A living fluid, it had eaten its way into the vehicles, unable to affect the metal but easily digesting the plastics. It had digested everything soft. Silently and painlessly, it had dissolved the men from Heaven.

Iorga realized that the blight which was laying waste the forest was not the agent which had brought death to the convoy. It occurred to him while he stood and looked that what had happened was reciprocal. The men from Heaven had brought the blight which destroyed the plants. The protoplasmic predator which lived on the plants had moved, instead, to the invaders and their vehicles. Poison—the strongest poison—had destroyed them in a matter of hours. Against a liquid life-form with such corrosive power they had no conceivable defense.

Iorga backed away, and returned to his companions.

"We must move," he said. "Quickly. We must escape the region of the blight, or we will die with the forest. We must not eat, or sleep, or be still."

"Everything is dying," said Huldi. The note of fatalism in

her voice suggested that she had no faith in her ability to except herself from the condition.

"We must go quickly," said Iorga.

They went quickly, and carefully. As they passed by the stricken vehicles, they trod with great care, avoiding the silver gel wherever they could see it. They did not run, but they moved swiftly, and when they were tired they continued to move.

Eventually, they felt the pressure of time building up inside them. They needed rest, they needed food and water, but they dared not stop while everything around them was dead or dying. Their minds became confused, and the seconds slowed to become painful. Many hours passed—and, for once, they were *conscious* of their passing—before they began to outdistance the spread of the viruses that contingent Delta had seeded before meeting its death. But they did, eventually, come once again into land that was free of the blight.

They continued to follow the road of stars, and death followed them, at its own pace.

19.

If the Euchronian Plan, in all its languid majesty, may be considered as a sequence of moves in a game of Hoh, then the i-minus project may be seen as a crucial ploy within the overall strategy: an attempt to "promote" the pieces with which the game was played, an attempt to force human evolution in a calculated manner.

Euchronian history, as represented to the citizens of the Millennium, depicted the Plan triumphant and the commitment of the people to it as absolute. The reality had been somewhat different. The builders had never been happy under the Plan. History admitted that—it was not the purpose of the builders to be happy, but to build so that their descendants should inherit the promised land. Where history evaded the truth was in its suggestion that the builders were always content to be unhappy, to suffer hardship, to give over their entire lives to the great work. They were not. Their willingness to devote themselves entirely to the Plan was perhaps never absent, but it was also never constant. The Movement had its overt rebels, and even within the most devout believers there sheltered doubts, and momentary revolts against the tyranny of the Plan. How could it have been otherwise?

In order that the Plan should not falter, that it should be certain of successful completion, the Euchronians had found themselves required to encourage commitment, and finally to compel it. They found human nature to be against them, and they determined to change human nature. The world which was to be the end-point of the Euchronian Plan had to be worthy of its builders, but its builders also had to be worthy of the world they were to create.

The aim of the Euchronian Movement was education. It wanted to teach its people to be perfect Euchronians. But somehow, the people always seemed to learn different priorities, different standards and different attitudes to stand beside those taught by Euchronia and conflict with them.

The Euchronian psychologists decided that the extra educational input was somehow innate. They theorized that the instinctive programming of the individual was against them. They came to believe that while men were asleep and dreaming, while the programs of the mind were being re played, rehearsed and continually readjusted, the social conditioning which they sought to impose was being infected by instinctive programming and weakened or subverted. To combat this, they designed the i-minus agent—a selective genetic inhibitor which prevented all innate input into dreaming. The programs which were replayed in the dreams of Euchronia's citizens were those supplied by Euchronia. Theoretically, the psychologists decided, this should lead to perfect social adjustment and effective education.

They were half-right. The instinctive input was muted. But the external input could not be completely unified. The undercurrents of dissatisfaction, of dissent, of rebellion, were sustained—not by constant instinctive reinforcement but simply because of their presence in the social reality at the commencement of the project. The plurality of opinions and the multiplicity of ideas could not be destroyed by the i-minus agent.

But the i-minus agent, administered in secret to all of Euchronia's citizens, did what was required of it—it ensured the safety of the Plan and the Movement until the completion of the platform and the declaration of the Millennium. The pieces in the game of Hoh *were* changed, and their inner life was significantly affected. The children of Euchronia did not become children of Reason, but they were very much the children of Intellect. Perhaps for the first time, civilized men broke free from their animal origins, from the evolutionary legacy of mind. They freed themselves from their nightmares.

Then the nightmares came back.

Joth Magner, by escaping into the Underworld where he ate food and drank water which were both innocent of the i-minus agent, recovered the old input—the instinctive input preserved genetically through the relatively few generations which had passed since the beginning of the project. Other men, however, found a new input—a telepathic input receptive to radiation broadcast by the Children of the Voice, or their Souls. Carl Magner was the first, but—at least potentially—there had been many more. The blast of radiation accompanying Camlak's translocation from his own space into the parallel space where the Gray Souls lived had activated that input in thousands of brains, perhaps millions, in both the Overworld and the Underworld.

The i-minus project was wrecked. The "promotion" of the pieces in the game of Hoh was rendered meaningless. A new evolution was taking place.

20.

Heres could not help staring at Sisyr's fingers. He felt a lump in his throat, and there seemed to be an incipient tremor welling up inside him. He had to hold himself rigid, and he knew that if his concentration relaxed for a moment some part of him—perhaps his hands—would begin to shake uncontrollably.

The room was featureless. No part of the cybernet extended herein, neither sensors nor receptors. The walls enclosed nothing but empty space. It was deep within the plexus, but in a real sense it was "outside"—beyond the host-machine, a hole in the artificial organism. There was a heavy chair, to which Sisyr was secured by steel manacles. There were men on either side of him. Confronting him were Heres, Luel Dascon and Acheron Spiro. Heres was in control. Only Heres knew what was happening.

Dascon had never seen the alien before. He had never thought about him. He considered the alien a kind of semi-mythical creature, in whose existence he had never quite been able to bring himself to believe. He found Sisyr rather repulsive.

Spiro found the alien frightening. The concept of an immortal creature was, to him, a rather frightening one in itself. Spiro feared death and disease and injury, just as Heres did, and felt an overwhelming bitterness when forced to contemplate the reality of a creature to whom these things meant nothing. Like Heres, Spiro was apprehensive, but not for the same reasons.

"I have considered the demands which we have to make," said Heres. "In the end, I decided that there are two—only two—which we must put to you. Firstly, you must tell us how to protect our minds against any further invasion of the kind which we have once experienced. Secondly, you must tell us how we can destroy the Underworld in the minimum possible time. We must have a date that we can publish, and a method we can be sure of. There must be no more deaths in the Underworld."

Sisyr remained silent. Not a muscle in his face moved in the slightest. A minute dragged by.

"Well?" said Heres.

"There is no way to protect your mind against invasion," said Sisyr, "and the Underworld cannot be destroyed."

"Your civilization is a good deal more advanced than ours," said Heres.

"Your concept of advance has no meaning," Sisyr stated flatly.

"Your technology, then," persisted the Hegemon. "You have the technology to achieve things we cannot."

"We are different," said the alien.

"You can do things we cannot."

"Yes. But we are not miracle-workers. We cannot do everything."

"I think you're lying," said Heres. "I think that you know the means to destroy the Underworld, but that you will not help us."

"There is no way," said Sisyr, "but I will not help you in the attempt."

"What would you have us do?" broke in Spiro. "You say that we cannot protect ourselves. What can we do but fight? We have no alternative."

Sisyr made no answer.

Heres began to speak again, but Dascon cut him off. "Wait," he said. "Let us try to be clear about one thing. When this... shall we call it a mental invasion?...occurred, did you experience anything?"

"Yes," said Sisyr.

"You were too far away," said Heres. "It can hardly have had any effect at all."

"Nevertheless," said Dascon, quickly, "you did experience something. A touch, perhaps, and no more—but something. Perhaps we can assume that what you experienced was not so very different from what some of us experienced. May I ask how you reacted to that experience? I ask this because it seems to me that we are talking at cross-purposes. What happened to us frightened us very badly. We feel the need to act quickly and definitely. But you, apparently, do not feel the same way. Why not? Perhaps you have known things like this before. Perhaps you simply do not understand the character of our reaction."

"Perhaps," said Sisyr. "Almost certainly. I cannot feel as you feel. But how can I begin to explain how I feel? There is no way."

"We have concepts in common," said Dascon. "You can use our language. Its words must have meaning for you. Tell us, in words, what the experience meant to you. Did it frighten you?"

"No."

"Surprise, then? Were you startled?"

"No."

"You were expecting something of the kind?"

"It was unexpected. But I was not surprised."

"Then you have felt something like it before. Before you came to Earth. Something similar has happened to you in the past?"

Sisyr paused before answering. Finally, he said: "Similar... perhaps. But not the same. The nature of the force involved was known to me. The precise nature of the manifestation was not."

Dascon rapped the table with his clenched fist. "At last," he said, "we begin to get somewhere. You know the nature of the force involved. Do you know how it was generated?"

"An aberration in space. Perhaps you would call it a knot, or a lesion. The physical nature of the event I am familiar with, even if I do not understand it as some of my race might. But what it means in terms of your minds—that I cannot know. I do not know how you can isolate yourselves from another such occurrence. I do not believe that there is any way that you could. How can you shield yourselves against the force of gravity? There is no way."

Dascon looked sideways at Heres, and shrugged.

"If what you say is true," said Heres, "then we have no alternative but to destroy the sources, or potential sources, of this force. We must destroy the Underworld. Can you see the logic of that?"

"Your logic, perhaps," said Sisyr. "Not mine."

"You ask us to do nothing. To hope that the thing will not occur again, or—if it does—to suffer it. To have our minds destroyed."

"Perhaps it is not destruction," said the alien.

"What does that mean?" demanded Spiro.

"I do not know what it means—to you. You cannot know what it means to me. If you wish, I will try to explain."

"There is no time," said Heres. "We do not want explanation. We want help. We demand help. You say the Underworld cannot be destroyed, but we know that is not so. In time, we could do it. But we do not have the time available to us. We need the aid of your technology to speed up the task. You must tell us how to make our methods more efficient, how to make equipment which will do the job more quickly. All we want from you now is the same help that you gave our ancestors. We want you to improve our means of production, refine our methods. Simply help us in the task we have set ourselves. You owe us this."

Sisyr shook his head deliberately. The mimicking of the human gesture seemed to Heres somehow profane.

"We can compel you!" he said, anger flooding his voice.

To this, Sisyr said nothing.

Heres half-rose from his chair. "You don't die," he said, harshly. "But we can kill you. Are you immune to pain? We have the power to *force* you. You must see that."

Dascon had seen this coming, but Spiro, strangely enough, had not. It was Spiro who had become angry along with Heres, but as Heres threatened the alien it was Spiro who recoiled, who began suddenly to sweat. It was Spiro who was nauseated.

Sisyr's pale blue eyes stared steadily into Heres' gray ones.

"You could kill me," conceded the alien. "Though you would not find it easy. I am not immune to pain. But you cannot use either the threat of death or the administration of pain to force me to go against my will. It cannot be done."

"I don't believe you," said Heres.

"It is so," replied Sisyr. "I am immortal—at least potentially.

I endure. I feel pain, but if necessary I can endure pain. Forever, if necessary. That is what immortality means. I can be killed, if every cell in my body is destroyed, but I am not afraid of being killed. One is only afraid of the inevitable. You must understand that I am not like you. You cannot force me to do anything. No matter what you may do."

Heres became suddenly conscious that his hands were trembling. He could not control them. He realized then that he *did* believe the alien: that he was convinced of his own helplessness.

21.

The driver brought the truck to a halt some twenty feet short of the bridge. Germont raised himself to as high a vantage as the canopy would permit, and looked carefully all around. There was no sign of life.

There was, in fact, no apparent need for suspicion at all. Thus far, in moving into the heart of the inhabited country, Germont's expeditionary force had met with no hostility whatsoever. The crop-spraying had proceeded unhindered at five townships. There had been no outwardly aggressive action on either side. Now, for the first time, the rough road of the Children of the Voice had led them to a waterway too wide for the vehicles to cross. There was a bridge, but a bridge built by the Shaira for their own use. It did not look as if it would take the weight of one of the armored cars, and there was no reason to suppose that it would. Somewhere back in the convoy there was equipment capable of erecting a bridge from scratch, or—if it proved more convenient—strengthening the structure that was there already. But for the first time the party would be obliged to stop for a moderate period of time while its personnel were working outside, unprotected by armor plate, in what was theoretically enemy territory.

"If they've only been waiting their chance," said the driver dourly, "this is it."

Germont spared him a sour glance.

The river flowed at the bottom of a valley. It was not deep, but it was deep enough for the slopes on either side to be difficult ground on which to maneuver. Germont could see no more than a mile in any direction—considerably less in the direction they had come, where the slope was steepest and the top of the hill closest. The slopes were covered with matted vegetation rather like bracken, with occasional tall clumps of quasi-dendrites. The whole aspect of the plant life here seemed different from the weird conglomerate forests of the darklands and the moist confusion of the Waste away to the north. Here, the general appearance the vegetation was much closer to moorland and heath. Only on close inspection were the basic structures of the environment revealed to be alien.

Germont sent one truck back to the crest of the hill, and instructed its commander to keep scanning with the search-light. Then he moved his own vehicle off the road while those carrying the pontoons and hawsers came to the fore. He sent men out to both left and right, telling them to hold fixed positions and signal to one another at regular intervals. A third party went across the bridge.

To demonstrate his faith in the invulnerability of his force he got out himself—the first time he had done so since he had seen the doctor shot on the road of stars—to supervise the operation.

He walked out on to the wooden bridge, where the man in charge of the pontoon team, Gunn Spurner, was already inspecting the possibilities. As he set foot—somewhat gingerly—on the native structure, he heard Spurner giving orders to his men, waving them off the bridge and away to the left. He directed them primarily with gestures. They moved quickly—perhaps a little too quickly, keen to play out their parts and put on a show of efficiency. As Germont drew level with Spurner the noise of the drills was already beginning.

"No good?" said Germont, pointing down at the bridge.

Spurner shrugged. "Good enough," he said. "Not really wide enough. It's easier to start from scratch. If we used this one, we'd only smash it up. Wouldn't be much use the next time."

"Next time?"

"When we come back."

Germont shook his head. "We'll go straight through to another exit," he said. "If necessary, they'll take the men up and abandon the vehicles. We aren't going back."

There was a moment's silence, while they reflected on the meanings implicit in the statement.

"Do you know what happened to the Deltas?" asked Spurner, quietly. His voice was flat and apparently unconcerned.

"Not yet," said Germont.

Another silence inevitably followed this statement. Germont moved to the edge of the bridge, now convinced that the structure was secure, and looked down into the water. It was flowing so slowly that its movement was hardly detectable. The water was murky and carried a heavy, oily scum.

"Foul," he commented. "I wonder why."

"Effluent?" suggested Spurner.

"I don't think so. We don't expel waste in this area, or anywhere upriver."

"The water must be ours," Spurner pointed out. "It doesn't rain here. Not ever. If it weren't for our water management there wouldn't be any life here at all. If we only tipped it all straight back into the sea this place would have been desert thousands of years ago."

"It's not as easy as that," said Germont. "We can only exert a certain amount of control over the water flow. We don't rule the rainfall. And even if we could...enough would get through. There'd always be enough. We could poison a lot of the water as it passed through the ducts in the platform on its way down here...but there'd still be enough. Enough water, not enough poison. The blight is the best way. The quickest way."

As he spoke, Germont moved along the bridge, still looking down at the water. He was tempted to reach down and dangle his gloved hand in the turbid liquid, testing its texture, but he dared not. He wondered vaguely whether there was anything alive in there. Obviously, by the way the water flowed turgidly and glutinously, there was a great deal of weed, but were there fish? Or crocodiles? He breathed deeply, trying to suck the air through his filter-mask in larger, more satisfying drafts. It felt good to be walking again, unconfined by the steel walls, able to stand up straight. After the first moments had passed, he no longer felt exposed, fearful of what might happen at any moment. He no longer anticipated the whiplash movement of an arrow, the cry of shock and pain that had barely escaped the doctor's lips before he died. This was a different environment—starlit, and far less eerie.

He turned to look back, to look at Spurner, still standing some five or six yards away on the bridge, to watch the men working with enthusiastic patience to get hawsers slung across the river and the pontoon units strung out to provide a road for the armored cars. He looked up at the slopes, and waited for the occasional, unsteady winking of the lights by which the soldiers signaled to one another that all was well.

He was suddenly struck by the oddness of the protective garments which the men wore. Here, where the stars were clustered and the light well-scattered, the suits tended to glint and gleam as the men inside them moved. The plastic was not really shiny, but it was smooth enough to reflect, almost in the same way that the silvery scum on the river reflected as slow, tedious ripples wound their way away from the bank where the men were working. Once, Germont had seen film of men walking on the moon, in thick, shiny suits. His own men wore filters instead of vast domed helmets, and their suits hung slack because there was no excess pressure inside, but there was something of the same quality about their aspect and appearance.

We might as well be on the moon, he thought. Or Mars...or a world of another star. The air here is our air, and the water is the waste from our world. Nevertheless, we are aliens. We come wrapped up in our fragments of the real world—the world above. We dare not face this world on its own terms.

He had to back off to let men carrying the hawsers pass him, to begin work on the far bank. Spurner joined him again, and they stood together watching the work proceed.

"Looks like everything's all right," commented Spurner.

"Of course," agreed Germont, sounding and feeling anything but completely sure of himself.

"They seem to be scared to death of us," went on the other man. "They daren't come near. What do you think they see us as? Gods from the sky? A supernatural visitation? They're bound to blame us for the blight, but they may take it philosophically—an act of fate over which they have no possible control."

Germont felt suddenly angry. "Have you looked at them?" he demanded. "While we cut slowly through their fields, they stand on their walls and watch us. Have *you* watched *them*? Do they seem to you like people in the presence of their gods or their demons? They look to *me* as if they know *exactly* what we are. They *know* what they're doing, and they know why. And I'm scared because I think they can stop us any time they like. We have the fire-power and the armor, but if they wanted to they could stop us dead in our tracks. I think they're going to kill us all."

Spurner recoiled. Not only did he make no reply, but he searched his mind assiduously for a way to change the subject. This was not something he cared to think about.

Germont did not wait for him to find something to say. Instead, he went back across the bridge to his own vehicle, and swung himself back inside.

"I want six men," he said. "You three will do for a start. Pick up three from Alpha-two. Follow the road beyond the bridge for a couple of miles. I want to know what's there. Get back here in an hour. You'll have to move fast, but be careful. Now!"

The three men he had addressed were already suited and their weapons were beside them. They were reluctant to move out, and rather surprised that they had been ordered to, but they put their masks on hurriedly. Germont went forward to the cockpit. The driver looked at him critically.

"Sending men forward on foot is a bit dangerous, isn't it?"

he asked.

"Once we're across that river," said Germont, "we'll take up the hawsers and the pontoons for the next time. That means we can't get back across in a hurry. If they're waiting for us, they'll be just beyond that hill. And they'll be waiting for us to cut off our own retreat."

"And suppose that they are?" said the driver. "What then? Do we stay this side and run?"

"I wish we could," said Germont, in a low voice. "I really wish we could."

22.

Enzo Ulicon looked carefully at the image of Vicente Soron which presented itself to him on the screen.

"You look ill," he said.

"I am ill," said Soron. "It was the Underworld."

"Not an infection?"

"Oh, no. We can deal very easily with any infection picked up down there. It's not organic. It's just...general debility. Being down there for any period of time simply drains the life out of you. I just couldn't stand it any longer...not the second time. The doctor says that it's psychosomatic—that I'm thinking myself ill. But that doesn't make it any the less real. And when I found out about the corrosion...the shock."

"Yes," said Ulicon, feeling that further discussion of Soron's state of health was rather pointless. "That's not what I wanted to talk to you about. I thought that I'd take advantage of your recall to go over the matter of the creature's disappearance. We still can't piece together a reasonable account of what happened and why. I'm convinced that we've missed something and I'm trying to find out what it is."

"I've reported absolutely everything," Soron said. "I really don't want to discuss that any more. I'd rather be left alone. I'm bitterly regretting that I was involved in that particular incident."

"Please, Vicente," said Ulicon. "This is important."

"What do you want to know?"

"I want to know exactly what was administered to the creature. Some circumstance arising as a result of your handling of it allowed it to perform that disappearing act. So far as we know this is a unique event. It never happened before and it hasn't happened since. I must know *exactly* what you gave that creature."

"I made a list," said Soron, tiredly. "It's all there. I gave it a dose of the same anesthetic that was in the dart gun when it began to show signs of life, and I continued to shoot it full of the stuff as the dose continually wore off. The drug is a mixture, but all the constituents are fairly commonplace. We had nothing to feed it, so I administered intravenous shots of glucose. I also gave it some shots of ferric tartrate and phenylalanine to compensate for some of the metabolic side effects of the sedatives."

"That's all here," said Ulicon, referring to a printout in front of him. "We wonder if any of these things may have had some effect on the creature quite apart from the purpose for which it was given. If that were the case, which of these might it be?"

"That's ridiculous," said Soron. "The only substance that it wouldn't meet in its own environment is the anesthetic cocktail. The effect *that* had was perfectly obvious. It worked as it should. Certainly, there might have been side effects that don't occur in humans, but they'd be organic, metabolic effects. How could an anesthetic give the thing the ability to teleport itself?"

"I don't know," said Ulicon, "but *something* did." Soron shook his head.

"It may have been an innate ability that was simply triggered by the drug," persisted Ulicon. "If that's so we need to know what the trigger was. Now an anesthetic acts on the brain—it causes lack of consciousness. The drugs in the mixture act in slightly different ways—some suppress neural activity, others can have slight psychedelic properties. Our only method of trying to find a likely candidate is logic—this isn't something we can play about with. We must be sure at the outset that you didn't administer a different kind of sedative at some point, or any other kind of drug. Are you certain that your list is complete?"

"Absolutely," said Soron. "The only thing the rat had except for those drugs is water."

"Water?"

"We let it regain semi-consciousness a couple of times. It drank a lot of water—those sedatives can give you a burning thirst, you know."

Ulicon said nothing. A pause grew and extended.

"What's the matter?" said Soron.

"Nothing. Just a thought. Thanks, Vicente. That's all I wanted to know."

"It's a wild goose chase," said Soron. "Believe me. You're on the wrong track."

Ulicon switched off the circuit. He scratched his chin, and murmured: "Eureka."

23.

While Nita slept, she dreamed. She had always dreamed, and each time she slept there had always been a time when the dreams were unnaturally deep, and unnaturally real. In these deep dreams the shadow of her Gray Soul was ever-present. Sometimes, it would talk to her, but on most occasions it was content to wait. There was something valuable, something inexpressively pleasant, in simply being together, in meeting and almost touching. They never could touch, because of the interface which lay between them, the surface of one mind within another.

The closeness of dreams was something which affected consciousness only transiently. To retain an awareness of the experience special measures had to be taken. The priests of the Children of the Voice were able to participate in the communion more or less at will, by the aid of mental discipline. The others generally needed drugs to heighten their awareness, to give them more freedom within their minds and in the inner space delimited by their minds. Without the pulp and the gum prepared by the priests and issued at the Communion of Souls, Nita and the common people among the Children of the Voice remained consciously unaware of the experience of Soul-nearness to a considerable extent. Nita was always aware that there was more to her inner life than she could remember or command, that there were worlds beyond the narrow fiction which she constructed and called her self. This mystical aspect of her inner life was continually reinforced by the fragments of experience which remained when her deep dreams dissipated and her mind returned to the surface of consciousness. Sometimes, one such fragment of memory would survive intact—a flake of secret reality, a rivet of insight—and would continue to haunt her waking mind thereafter, its meaning perpetually out of reach but its significance sharp and clear.

So it was when, without warning, Camlak came to her in her dream.

He was often present in her dreams, of course. He was always in her mind. But this time, while she slept very deeply, her body and mind exhausted by the long flight from the death that was devouring the blacklands, it was the real Camlak who came to her. He was with the Gray Soul, beyond the interface. She could not quite reach out and touch him, but she could see him, in a strangely shadowed way, and she heard his words.

When she woke again, committing herself totally to the external world, to the self she had created for facing that particular aspect of infinity, she could not remember his speech in full. The words he had used could not be seized and held by her waking mind—they ran through its crevices like quicksilver. But the meaning remained with her, unclear, but nevertheless tangible...memorable...real....

He had spoken to her not of a world, but of worlds. He had spoken of bodies becoming shadows, of minds becoming liquid creatures unconfined by *shape* and dimension, creatures into which time *dissolved* and *flowed.* He had spoken of clouded mountains holding everlasting sunset, of white oceans like liquid ashes, of darkness and light, of.... She lost the images even as she tried to recall them. In her world, they made no sense. In her words, they had no meaning. Only within the tissue of the dream had they been able to become real, just for a few moments. The concepts were beyond the boundaries of her own being, outside the horizons of her mind.

But what reality could not snatch away from her was the assurance that Camlak was alive, that the Overworld had not destroyed him, that somehow he had transcended even Heaven and Hell.

24.

"I came as soon as I learned what had happened," said Rypeck. "I was shocked. Please believe me when I tell you that if it were only within my power...this is a terrible thing. They simply do not realize what they have done.... What they are doing."

Sisyr did not react in any way to Rypeck's obvious distress. His hands were no longer manacled—that symbolic gesture had proved quite pointless, and Heres had directed that the offensive objects should be removed. But the alien was still held in the featureless room—an absolute captivity, in a world which relied so totally on its electrical senses, where life was conducted and mediated by mechanical extensions of the hand and brain.

As the silence lengthened, Rypeck added: "I'm sorry."

"The crisis will pass," said Sisyr. "This is a transient thing."

"They are lost," said Rypeck, sitting down. His body seemed to fold up as he relaxed himself—perhaps overrelaxed himself. He was tired. "They have no idea how to react or what to do next. They feel an unreasonable urgency which simply cannot be assuaged. I don't think they will harm you.

Sisyr said nothing.

"We talked about this," said Rypeck. "Such a short time ago. I asked you what would happen if the Movement asked your help again. We talked about the consequences of action and the consequences of inaction. Your answers seemed to me to be unclear."

"Within your contexts," said the alien, "they were unclear. They still are."

"But there was one thing that you said," Rypeck mused. "You said that while we saw two worlds, you only saw one. You saw Earth, Underworld and Overworld, as an integrated whole. What do you see now? A world tearing itself apart? That, I think, is how I am beginning to see it. A world involved in the single-minded business of self-destruction."

"There is no self-destruction," said Sisyr softly. "Only self-repair."

"Repair?"

"Self-change, if you prefer."

Rypeck shook his head. He wore a bitter smile. "We have never preferred self-change. We preferred stability. Total order. The state of parasitism. That was our Utopian dream. We still cling to it. We *prefer* self-satisfaction, self-sterilization...the homogeneity of life."

"Something," said the alien, "which can be all too easy to find."

The remark seemed to Rypeck to be unnaturally cryptic. He looked hard at Sisyr.

"What must you think of us?" he said. "As you look out upon us from your lofty heights of eternity. Are we ants surrendering everything to the greater glory of the anthill, unaware that the land where our universe exists is about to be plowed up, drowned by a tidal wave, swallowed up by the Earth? Is that what you see? Is all our human vanity so utterly ridiculous?"

Sisyr shook his head.

"How do you see us?" demanded Rypeck. "You have seen us through eleven thousand years. You have seen us pour our lives, our being, into the construction of this almighty metal anthill. You have helped us find and use the materials with which to make it fulfill our dreams. To me, Euchronia is everything. It is my universe—the past when Euchronia did not exist is to me unimaginable, composed of dreams. But you know how little that is. You have *dabbled* in the building of my world. It has been a mere pastime, the tiniest fraction of your life. To me, it means everything, to you, almost nothing. Tomorrow will be the end of our world, but *your* world is infinite, eternal. It faces no crises, no climacticon. Do we seem to you to be absurd?"

"No."

"I don't believe you."

"It is true. Believe me, I am far more involved in your world, in your affairs, than you imagine. This Earth is not my toy, not merely a momentary distraction. I am not a god, despite the fact that I will not die. You read too much into that simple fact. Perhaps your people mean no more to me than the Children of the Voice, but they mean no less. You are real, you are human. You are so like me in so many respects, so unlike in others—but I see the like as well as the unlike. Please believe me when I say that I *care* about what is happening to you and to your world. But I cannot help in the way that Heres understands help. If there is any kind of salvation, you must find it yourselves. There is nothing I can do."

Rypeck's eyes played over a white wall, as if searching for some tiny crack to distort its smoothness, its emptiness.

"I believe you," he said.

"Thank you," replied the alien.

"*Is* there any possible salvation?" asked the human.

"I cannot know," said Sisyr. "In your terms, I simply do not know what salvation is."

"The survival of the Overworld," said Rypeck. "The peace, the stability, the safety of our lives."

"Perhaps that can happen," said the alien. "For now. But is that salvation? For your children's children, forever and ever, is that salvation?"

"It's what we believe in."

"Beliefs change," said Sisyr. "They can never be constant. Don't you find that there always has to be something new to believe in, and that the beliefs you have are steadily eroded away?"

"I don't know," said Rypeck. "Nobody does."

25.

"There's a barrier across the road," reported the spokesman for the party Germont had sent on across the bridge. "It's just beyond the crest of the hill. Not half a mile. It extends to either side in a rough semicircle, and ends up in the dense vegetation on the slope itself, over there, and there. It doesn't look like a barricade from here, but I think they've dumped stuff in between the clumps of vegetation. Once we're across the river, we're effectively hemmed in. Water behind us and the wall on all three sides. The barrier's all of a mile and a half long—it isn't something that was thrown up overnight. This is where they intend to stop us all right."

"How close did you get?" Germont demanded.

"Just close enough to see. We weren't about to go up and say hello."

"Did you see the rats?"

"No. But they were there. I could feel it. They're behind that barrier, I'll swear it."

"What's the barrier made of?"

"What passes for wood hereabouts, I think. The same sort of stuff that stands up straight on these slopes. It's high, but it can't be strong. The trucks would go through it like a knife. I guess."

"Then what's it for? If it's that soft it won't stop bullets?"

The spokesman shrugged. "To hide behind, I guess. Maybe it's the best they could do. Perhaps there's a ditch behind it—perhaps they hope we'll crash through and cripple the vehicles. What are we going to do?"

"Tell Dascon," snapped Germont. "Let's see if he has any ideas."

He went back to the communications panel, and relayed to Dascon exactly what the scout had told him.

Dascon was unimpressed. "You have the fire-power," he said. "Tear the barricade apart. Blast it out of the way."

"You wouldn't like to come down here and do it yourself?" said Germont.

"You're making a fool of yourself," replied the Councilor. "There's no need to be frightened of a lot of half-animal savages. I know you've lost men already, but that has no bearing upon the present situation. Leave a truck to hold the bridge, if you want your rear protected and an escape route assured."

"Thanks," said Germont. "Just stay close to that screen. You can watch through the cameras. At least, if anything does go wrong, you'll know what it is."

"I'm watching," said Dascon, his voice smooth, showing no trace of irritation because of Germont's bitterness.

By means of the camera eye on the front of the truck, Dascon watched as Germont's truck ventured on to the makeshift bridge, and lumbered across the slow-moving river to the opposite bank. As it ascended the hill Germont ordered the search-light and the machine gun manned, and Dascon watched the light pick out the crown of the hill as the truck rode up the slope. He heard Germont give instructions for Spurner to stay with the tail-end truck on the north side of the river.

In a matter of minutes the armored vehicle created the rise, and then Dascon saw the wall—just a loose assemblage of dead, dry vegetable matter piled up in a long, straggling line which arced away to present a concave arc to the lorries as they changed gear and sped forward. The lights from the other trucks joined Germont's searchlight, scanning the wall for signs of the enemy.

And then the wall became a wall of flame. At least a dozen lights, maybe more, were applied simultaneously. Either the material of the barricade had been soaked with some flammable liquid, or the dry stalks were very combustible indeed, because once started the flames sprang up with considerable eagerness.

The truck braked.

"Back off," commanded Germont. "Back off and let it burn itself out."

The vehicle was thrown into reverse, and the mechanical eye through which Dascon saw retreated steadily. The ribbon of flame extending across the viewfield seemed rather futile—a ridiculous gesture of defiance. But the eye was fixed. It looked forward, and it was locked into the frontal stare. As the truck pulled back to the crest of the hill, Dascon could see only the pall of thick, oily smoke that was already blotting out the electric stars beyond the barrier. But he heard

Germont's cry of anguish, and—though no words came to him—he guessed what had happened.

The Shaira had set fire to the river. The water was polluted, loaded with oil and alcohol. The scum on the surface was not vegetable, but mineral.

And Germont's trucks were trapped, ringed by fire. The fire could not burn for long—it would be a fast flare and little more. But the circle was tilted by the slope of the hill. As the air within the ring rose the hot gases from the surface of the river would be sucked inwards, up the slope. Inside the trucks, the men would have their own supply of oxygen, but the armored walls of the trucks would become red-hot in a matter of moments as the firestorm raged around them. If they got out, they would burn and choke. If they stayed in, they would be cooked.

All Dascon could see was the great cloud of smoke billowing over the crest of the hill. He was forced to cut out the sound that Germont's microphone was picking up. He simply could not stand to listen to it.

26.

"There's no way to prove what you say," said Rypeck.

"No way at all," agreed Ulicon. "But it fits. It's an answer which fits the question, and it's the only one we have which does. The water which we drink is recycled—not because we're short of water, but in order to conserve the i-minus drug. The drug has to be constantly supplied because it is excreted so easily, and so the supply is—to all intents and purposes—a closed circuit. The i-minus drug is not expelled into the Underworld with our waste except in the most minute quantities, and it is so easily degraded by strong alkali that virtually none of it will have got into the Underworld life-system. The concentration in our water is quite high—on the order of several parts per million. Quite enough to affect the creature if it drank a pint or two of Overworld water."

"We have no way of knowing what effect it might have had."

"But we have. The drug acted on the creature exactly as it was designed to act. It cut out the instinctive input into his dreaming. And left what? The input from his conscious mind—the memories and visual images which were the content of the telepathic broadcast, plus the other input—the input from *elsewhere*, from the Gray Soul. By cutting the instinctive input into the dream state, the i-minus agent made possible a closer contact between the creature and the thing which it called a soul than ever before. That's what made it possible for the creature to disappear—to go wherever it went, into the space where the Soul is."

"You think this Gray Soul is a real being, not just a mental archetype?" queried Rypeck.

"I do. It fits. The rat people are in telepathic contact with other beings, but the contact is blurred by the fact that it takes place in the same bodies within the brain that are involved with dream-sleep—the focus of the whole thing is probably the pons. Harkanter and Soron, quite unknowingly, made it possible for the creature to make much better use of that telepathic linkage."

Rypeck nodded slowly. "It's all very speculative," he said.

"But if it's true," persisted Ulicon, "then we have grounds for thinking—at least for *hoping*—that there won't be a recurrence.

Without the i-minus agent, the rat people might not be able to effect a similar contact. We might be *safe*—at least for a time. We have time to think, time to adjust, time even to adapt, if we must. Surely we can stop this mad panic!"

"I think it's gone too far."

"We must try."

"With this mass of conjecture? We need more than a chain of ideas to persuade people. Not Heres—we'll never persuade Heres—but the people who might be in a position to halt the panic if Heres can be removed. We need hard evidence, and there's no way to get it."

"There's one way," said Ulicon.

"Repeat the process?" said Rypeck, his lips forming a half-smile at the irony. "That's what we're trying to prevent."

"We could try to make a contact," said Ulicon. "We know that the potential exists in people as well as in rats. Carl Magner had that potential. And after the blast...I think there's a good many of us can now pick up the kind of leakage he did. Joth told us that in the village, they chewed plant pulp to help them communicate with their Gray Souls. We have specimens of that plant, courtesy of Harkanter's expedition. I think we should try it on a man."

"Who?"

"If he's willing, the man most likely to succeed. Joth Magner."

27.

Joth's first reaction, when they came to him with the proposition, was: "Why me?"

"Two reasons," Ulicon told him. "First, you are your father's son. We don't know that his ability or potential was heritable, but it seems at least possible that there was a genetic predisposition. Secondly, you were closest to Camlak when he disappeared. Whatever effect the event had on our minds, it will have been at a maximum in your case. The only other person with your qualifications is your sister. But you have extra advantages in that you know more than any of us about the kind of context into which any contact you do make is to be put. As well as being the most likely candidate to make the contact, you are the most likely one to make sense of it."

"And what will it prove if I do make contact?" asked Joth.

"What it may prove," Rypeck interposed, "depends very much on the nature of the contact itself. What we want is to convince ourselves that we are on the road to understanding— that we are beginning to come to terms with the events that have happened. But if we succeed in the experiment, there is no knowing what we may learn. Perhaps very little—I doubt that we are in a position to learn very much because we are so totally naive with regard to the implications of what is going on—but perhaps something very important."

"I want to help," said Joth. "You know that."

"But you're afraid," added Ulicon. "That's understandable."

"Suppose," said Joth, "that what happened to Camlak happens to me. We don't know that what he did was voluntary."

"We assume that you will retain a degree of control over what happens," Ulicon told him. "We think that it's unlikely that the contact will harm you. By your own evidence, the Children of the Voice are convinced that the intimacy with the Souls is a good thing, that the Souls are benign."

"Exactly what do you want to do?" asked Joth.

"We will inject into your veins an extract from the plant which you have identified as the one used by the villagers to stimulate contact during their Communion. We have tested it, and it seems to be harmless. Then we will induce deep sleep by direct electrical stimulation to the brain. With the encephalographic cyborg we can control the incidence of dream-sleep—can maintain or break it. The i-minus agent is already present in your body, but we will monitor its level continuously, and perhaps boost its concentration. We cannot monitor your dreams, of course, but we can stimulate retention within your own mind. We will always be able to wake you if you show any sign of physiological distress, but we will not do so unless we fear that you will come to some harm. We expect that the experience will be stressful to a degree.

"Perhaps there is one more thing that you ought to know, and that is that the experiment will be conducted without the knowledge or consent of Rafael Heres. In order to make it meaningful we will have to break the secrecy of the i-minus project. We have already told you that the agent exists—we must also inform the medical and scientific observers we coopt into the experiment. We intend to inform Abram Ravelvent and your own doctor, Joachim Casorati. Clea Aron will also be present, as the only other member of the upper echelons of the Movement who seems likely to be sympathetic toward what we are doing. There may well be others in attendance. In a sense, what we are doing is betraying the system of the Close Council, and Heres may wish to construe this as treason against the Movement, *if* Heres is still in power when the experiment takes place."

"There's a chance he may be stopped?" asked Joth.

"A chance," said Ulicon.

"Welcome to the revolution," added Rypeck, drily.

"Well," said Joth, quietly. "I've already been on one journey through Hell. Wherever this one takes me...I'll survive.

"I'll do it."

28.

Rafael Heres was a man devoted to—and committed to—the principle of a pattern in life. His mind saw Hoh as a perfect analogue of Euchronia, and Euchronia as a perfect analogue of Hoh. Winning, to him, meant the imposition of a pattern, the enforcement of stability, and his idea of fulfilment in life was control over the pattern of life.

He had a tremendous capacity for finding answers to problems of great complexity (or what appeared to be great complexity), but the basis of this ability was not really intellectual acuity so much as an unbreakable faith in the fact that all problems, no matter how complex, had a single answer which would impose the sacred conformity to pattern. He was not, in any sense, a precise analyst of problems, merely an accomplished solver. Like Alexander confronted with the Gordian knot, he was a great believer in pragmatic solutions: if a knot would not yield to logic, then it must yield to force, it must be severed, even if it could not be untied.

This insight into Heres' character goes a long way to explaining his utter helplessness in the face of the circumstances following the Overworld's vision of Hell. Here was a knot which would not yield to the sword. It could not be forced to comply with Heres' assumptions about Knots. There was no way that the Euchronian pattern to which Heres was committed could be reconstituted, but Heres was incapable of admitting this. And so the very source of his erstwhile success was the instrument of his total failure. The faith which had served so well in other circumstances now showed itself to be, in the ultimate analysis, inadequate, and even absurd.

When Luel Dascon came to him and reported that the expeditionary forces in the Underworld were meeting with failure on every front, and asked him to recall the remainder in order to save lives, Heres came face to face with his own fallibility. He saw the negative counterpart to the self-image which, according to the mirror of his mind, had always been the "fairest in the land."

"Zuvara's report," said Dascon, "indicates that the viruses are not one hundred percent effective, and that their spread is not so rapid as might be desired. The implications of his results, he claims, are ambiguous insofar as our declared program is concerned. Provided that the seeding is heavy enough, there is no way that the higher life-forms in the Underworld can survive the consequent disruption of their ecology. However, such a seeding would have to continue actively on a large scale for many years. The extinction of the people of the Underworld cannot be regarded as imminent, even in the limited areas where heavy seeding has so far taken place.

"The force now commanded by Gunn Spurner following Jacob Germont's death has been reunited, but over half the vehicles and men have been lost. The force is no longer proceeding south, but is retreating through the blighted country already seeded. The people of this region are migrating south, and we have evidence which suggests that the rat people are fighting the spread of the plague by burning the blighted areas. The spread of the viruses by wind, water and animal is being limited by this policy, though not completely stopped.

"The corrosion of the supporting structures of our own world discovered by Vicente Soron is, in some places, advanced enough to be a danger. The platform is not threatened by small-scale collapses, so far as we can tell, but stress and strain are building up in certain regions which may result in damage to systems. The conclusion here is that intercourse between Overworld and Underworld must be reinstituted on a worldwide basis. The repair of the platform's supporting structures must, from now on, be regarded as a priority. Bases like Zuvara's must be established on a permanent basis in many areas. To some extent, their continued existence must depend on their ability to withstand attack not simply from the subhuman inhabitants, but also from the kind of life-form which destroyed the Delta contingent of Germont's force. Identification of this organism is at present tentative, only mechanical devices having so far been sent to the scene of the disaster."

"Is that all?" whispered Heres.

"There's a great deal more," said Dascon. "But these are the most vital points."

"And what conclusions do *you* draw?"

"We must go back into the Underworld on a big scale," said Dascon. "That's vital. The idea we have been nursing that our own activities down there can be kept to a minimum no longer seems tenable. We must conclude that the Planners made a mistake when they sought to shut out all the problems posed by the surface by sealing it up and ignoring it. The Plan must be continued—perhaps on the kind of lines which you proposed in your program for a Second Plan. If we are to begin the reclamation of the surface with the extirpation of the life-system currently dominant there, then we will obviously have to make the extirpation a long-range objective rather than a short-range one. The question is: how can the people be reconciled to these ends. It won't be easy to persuade them to abandon their Millennium and go back to work. Not this kind of work—dangerous and dirty. Our citizens were born the children of a dream—the ultimately privileged. It isn't going to be easy to take that privilege away, especially in the current climate of stark terror. All over the world there are people barricading themselves into their houses, trying to requisition supplies for two years or twenty years from the cybernet, because they simply have no confidence that the cybernet is still going to be working next year or next month—no confidence that society will still be functioning next year or next month. All over the world, people are beginning to exempt themselves from Euchronia, trying to retreat into their own tiny corner of it, which they hope they can sustain by their own efforts forever. And in the meantime, we may lose our minds. Tomorrow, or the next day. Not one of us can claim control of his own sanity, his own inner being. Our quasi-Utopian order no longer means a thing.

"In order to survive at all, we of the Overworld have to redis-cover commitment—a commitment far more difficult than that which the original Movement fought for. We cannot offer the same assurances they could. Perhaps we can no longer offer even the *hope* of Euchronia. We can only try. We must do what we can."

"Sisyr is to blame," said Heres. Dascon had not expected the remark. It seemed to him to be a non sequitur. He had expected an affirmation of determination, support for his own verbally expressed conviction of the need to carry on. Dascon had always looked to Heres for confirmation of his own Euchronian cant—for the ultimate faith which he, in the final analysis, did not have. But Heres' conviction had come to a dead end. Suddenly, it was no longer there. It is always the deepest faith of all which submits to instantaneous evaporation, when its weakness is finally admitted.

"Sisyr kept the Underworld alive," Heres went on, when Dascon failed to reply. "He nurtured it in order that it could become our enemy. While he pretended to help the Plan, he sowed the seeds of Euchronia's destruction. He never intended that the Plan should succeed. He is the destroyer. All this time, through hundreds and thousands of years, he has been playing a game with us. It was never his intention that we should attain our ends. He has cheated a whole world."

"It's not so," said Dascon. "It can't be. He only wanted to keep both worlds alive. Isn't that *right*? Isn't that the proper way? In a game of Hoh, the ideal is for everyone to win."

"No!" said Heres. "He *never* intended that both worlds should become viable. He never intended that the Overworld should succeed. He has said so. He has confessed that he always knew our aims to be unattainable. He knew, because he made it so."

For the first time, it was Heres that looked to Dascon for confirmation, for justification. He expected it, for in all the years that Heres had known Dascon, he had seen him as little more than an echo, a testament to his own ability to be unfailingly correct.

But now Dascon said nothing, because for the first time Heres had failed to stand full-square with Euchronian ideology. For the first time, Heres spoke as a Eupsychian, and there was nothing left to believe in. Nothing at all.

29.

The stars stood still in the sky. Bright, clearly defined, pearl-white. The land they illuminated was likewise sharply defined, but somehow unreal and insubstantial, almost two-dimensional. The shapes were shadows, with the thinness of shadows. Bright illusions stood forth while realities hid, cloaked in darkness.

At one moment he experienced the world as though he were floating in midair, looking out and across the bleak panorama of the realms of Tartarus; and in another he felt himself huddled in the slime, with the touch of the cold, foul earth creeping into his flesh as though licking at him, dissolving him, consuming him. There was sweat on his body, perhaps in the external world as well as the microcosmic existence of the dream.

He sensed the presence of the Children of the Voice, not through hearing or seeing, but through some mystic sense of collective being: a transcendental sense, the property, perhaps, of the fourfold vision. He was aware of the Children *en masse*, as a quasi-hive organism, perpetually growing and dying by degrees, but he was also aware of stresses within the whole— tensions and repulsions, the ceaseless effort of exemption, of isolation. The identity of the species seemed, from Joth's Godlike viewpoint, to be in a state of constant flux, like a chemical reaction in virtual equilibrium, with associations constantly forming and breaking down. But, as well as being outside and above, Joth was also inside and below—if his seeing eye was Godlike, it was also wormlike—and in himself he felt the ebb and flow of their existence. Their fear was his fear, their dream was his dream.

As he drifted in space, so he began to drift in time. He felt himself caught, as though by a rapid current, and suddenly hurled into a dark corridor, as though falling—but falling *through*, not down.

The stars were whirled away with him—they did not leave him but they lost their roundness, like teardrops becoming streaks of silver. He moved as though through a sleeve of shooting stars.

He began to be overwhelmed by a black absence of any sense of direction, any sense of speed, any sense of distance or location.

He was not afraid. There was no conscious element in the psychophysiological reaction which entrapped him, and which was shuttling him through the chaos of his inner world—not the surface of consciousness, or even the underlying interface of dream and symbol, but the depths, the Tartarean realms. His movement, his senses and his being were in the grip of something more basic than essential self.

Joth ran, his heart pumping, his limbs sucking up energy from his physical core. His eyes reflected the whirligig gleam of the stars, but what he saw....

The Star King, dancing...night, decked with painted stars, the pace of the dance slowing as the rhythm of the drums grew turgid and the King himself could do no more than writhe, his dead legs unable to carry him, but still dancing, dancing....

The moist hand, lingering on and near his lips, his face hot and dry but the hand moist, tasting of...the lingering echoes of another dream, making his back rigid, the touch of madness....

An empty, derelict world...forests of shiny fungus hardened like wood...ground ridged and slick with bloated rhizoids and thick, matted humus, covered with cockroaches and small black beetles, and fleshy, squashy insects for eating with dirty, foul-smelling water thickened by slime...mud and puffballs and chytrids, monstrous edifices of mutually supportive hydroids... acid burning skin and mucous membrane...soft tentacles waving blindly in the air, sting-cells charged and constantly consuming, constantly sucking, constantly oozing through the morass....

Broth spooned into his mouth, gulped down and then vomited back, a thin, gray stream running down his cheeks and into the straw...and water pouring, running through him, over him, in baptism...and rebirth...out of the sickness and the wasting, and from the margins of death, the retreat of the world within and the world without...then the healing, the growing anew, the rebuilding and the self-repair, and the finding of fear...and love... *One lamp burning on a bracket in the wall, bricks and square stones showing through the plaster, cracks in the ceiling....*

The Star King, leaning forward, his belly touching her breasts...not breathing, not even alive...rigid...and then the Sun, striking like a snake...the flash of the axe as the blade caught and threw the starlight...the black mask rolling like a great black ball....

A great flat worm flopping like a rubber blanket, spitting out its guts...bubbling fountains of digestive juices...the villi of the blind intestine flapping like tiny grasping fingers...the deadly hiss of the acid in the algal scum...the worm, soft underfoot, writhing and sucking back its gut, sinking away into the ooze....

Blood, flooding the gray-green colors of the Earth-body...a torrent...a red sheen in the firelight, turning black...sliding the Night from the body, the Sun descending...bound together....

Metal eyes...are the men of your world made of metal?

All men are flesh and blood. I was hurt. I have been repaired....

A strip of darkness in the further sky...the black land...a thin line of light like a road of stars...echoes of an older civilization... the ruins of a city and the relics of an older mankind....

Torrents of thought, breaking in his mind...the Face of Heaven...the sound of the horn, the sudden face and the sudden fear....

The stars in the sky, pale and still...his whole body being eaten by pain while cockroaches moved over his body and he could not move...helpless and lost...mental continuity broken... tears in the corners of his eyes....

And then, quite suddenly, faces:

Huldi.

Nita.

Carl Magner.

Iorga.

Camlak.

Inside Camlak's eyes, a sudden flare of light. A scream, striking him down.

And....

In slow motion, Harkanter leveling the pistol and pulling the trigger. Harkanter's head, exploding....

Patterns blossoming on closed eyelids.

Firelit masks, bricks crumbling as a house burned, eaten away by flame, searching among the dead, the map, the road, the stillness and the death, and after that...nothing. No more.

Inside himself again, Joth as Joth, now still. The cone of stars no longer spinning, his world cut out in light and darkness, nothing more, the pattern nonsense but the shapes of darkness sharp and well defined.

His tongue felt suddenly very large. His mouth was grained, filled with grit and fur. His ribs felt like ice—a cage of ice around his heart. His bones, within him, felt cold. His belly was absolutely without feeling. There was a nearness about his body that made him aware of it, all save his gut, which was numb and void.

Then the light began to flicker, the radiance separating from the shadow. What had been a cocoon of two dimensions became a womb of three. There was a liquid cascade of light, and through the living matrix the shadows moved.

As though a curtain were drawn aside, to reveal to him a window...and beyond the window a gray world like fog and smoke. And in the window, a face.

Camlak's face.

30.

While Enzo Ulicon, Clea Aron, Abram Ravelvent, and Joachim Casorati supervised the attempt to awaken Joth Magner's latent telepathic ability, Rafael Heres was once again confronting Sisyr. Luel Dascon was with him.

"We have come to a decision," said Heres.

The word "we" was, in fact, empty of meaning. The only mind involved in the decision was Heres' own. Even Dascon had been excluded, and Dascon did not know what had been decided. In fact, Dascon was almost afraid of what Heres might have decided to do.

"What have you decided?" asked Sisyr, responding smoothly to Heres' obvious expectation.

"You must leave Earth," said the Hegemon. "You must leave and never return. Whatever your interests here, they are at an end. I do not profess to understand your actions during the time you have spent here, but the outcome of what you have done is intolerable. In the beginning, our predecessors asked you for help, and for this reason only we do not regard what you have done as completely hostile. But you cannot stay."

Sisyr's blue eyes stared first at Heres, and then moved to Dascon. Dascon felt their pressure, and was compelled to speak.

"It is best," he said.

"I will go," said the alien. "I will need time to prepare."

"You have twenty-four hours," said Heres.

"I need more," replied Sisyr.

"Why?"

"I am a long way from my home. I will have to make preparations for the journey. Interstellar journeys are measured in centuries, not in days. My ship has to be supplied, fueled, tested. It has been a long time."

"Very well," said Heres. "But you will understand that this work must be supervised."

"I do not understand," said Sisyr, flatly.

"We must be certain that there is no further interference," said Heres. "Your house is being searched. All records you have kept and all property which you have accumulated are being confiscated. We are not yet acquainted with the full range of your activities here, nor are we certain of their purpose, but no further activity must take place. You must make such preparations as are necessary, and depart with all due speed."

Sisyr said nothing, but gave a slight bow. There was no way of knowing whether this signaled acquiescence, or whether some irony was intended.

"Call in the police guard," said Heres, this time to Dascon.

Dascon opened the door. There were four policemen waiting outside. With them were a captain of police and Thorold Warnet. Dascon's eyes met Warnet's, and the recognition struck him cold. He felt the shock in his heart, a sharp, small pain that died quickly as he realized how little it meant.

Dascon stepped aside, holding the door wide for Warnet to

enter the room.

Heres was still facing Sisyr, and he did not turn instantly. It was only when the silence went on too long that he finally turned.

"Rafael Heres," said Warnet, almost lightly, "Luel Dascon. You're both under arrest."

The color drained from the Hegemon's face. He tried to speak, but the words simply would not come.

Warnet watched the effort which Heres put into trying to speak, and thought it very strange that there was real pain written in the other's face.

"We control the cybernet," said Warnet quietly. "We have the holovisual networks, and all the operative facilities. The take-over within the cerebral complex was orderly. There have been no casualties. We anticipate a good deal of intellectual dissent when we begin transmitting, but we have the machine, and the machine is the world. It will be a very quiet revolution."

"It's impossible," said Heres.

"It was inevitable." This whispered denial was Dascon's, not Warnet's.

"No one could get control of the cerebral complex," said Heres. "No one has the means. Only the Council could...."

"We have Council support," said Warnet quietly. "Not a majority, but enough. We have the police, and we have the technicians. It has been necessary to arrest perhaps ten or a dozen major councilors and technical supervisors. The rest either support us, or are prepared to stand by. Believe me, the structure of authority which supported you no longer exists. It dissolved, and it has been replaced."

"By whom?"

"That's not important. You must go to your home now, and you, Dascon, to yours."

"Rypeck," said Heres, slowly. "Ulicon...Sobol...they betrayed me. Even now...."

31.

Afterwards, Warnet said to Sisyr: "We still need your help. In fact, we need your help now more than we have ever needed it before."

"What kind of help?" asked the alien. Warnet heard bitterness in the tone, but whether the bitterness was really there, he could not tell.

"To make new plans," said Warnet. "Not a Plan, but plans. There will be no destruction of the Underworld."

Sisyr turned away. "I am tired," he said.

"You'd better go home," said Warnet. "We can contact you later. But we'd like you to join us...not the revolution, that is, but the new executive authority...whatever we put in place of the Council."

"There are men at my house," said the alien. "Searching...for what, I don't know. Are they under your command, now?"

Warnet shook his head. "We hold the brain of Euchronia. Outside, we have no actual authority, except that which extends through the cybernet. There may well be isolated groups and individuals who would rather stage their own counterrevolution than capitulate with circumstances. Would you rather stay here?"

"No."

"Then I'll send men back with you. If the men at your house are police, there'll be no trouble. If they're employees of the Movement, there's a chance they'll stay loyal to Heres, but I don't think they'll be very difficult to handle. You'll come to no harm."

"It's not for myself I'm afraid," said Sisyr, "but the house and its contents...."

"I'll do what I can," promised Warnet. "Thank you."

32.

"What's happened?" asked Clea Aron.

"He's still dreaming," said Casorati. "His brain is still active. But his body is now fully relaxed. The pons—the organ responsible for decoupling brain and motor nerve network during dreaming seems to have become suddenly more effective. Normally, there are quite distinct physical signs of dreaming—although the grosser effects of the motor nerves are damped, there is usually some muscular activity, and the physical aspects of emotional involvement are usually detectable. But Joth is physically stable to a considerable degree."

"Are you sure he's still dreaming?" asked Ravelvent.

"The encephalographic register hasn't settled into blackout rhythm."

"This could be it," said Ulicon.

"We've no way of knowing that," said Casorati. "No way at all."

"Isn't this the dangerous phase?" asked Clea Aron. "If something...untoward happens, it will be now."

"Perhaps," said Ulicon.

They waited. Their eyes watched the trace on the oscillograph as it flickered, amplitude and frequency changing—apparently at random.

"Isn't there any way of...decoding...that?" Again, the question came from the councilor.

"It's been tried," said Ulicon. "But there's no way. It tells us, in a vague sense, what's happening, but the signals aren't in any way a *language*. The patterns don't correspond to specific *thoughts*. We have some degree of control over what's happening, though. We can feed in signals of our own *via* the cyborg linkage. I can bring him back to dreamless sleep—shallow blackout or deep blackout—at any time. There is a state—the shallow state—in which we can communicate with him while he's still unconscious. It's rather like asking questions under hypnosis. He may be better equipped to tell us about the dreams in that state. The return of consciousness is bound to confuse him. The trouble is that we may not be able to make any sense out of what he says. If that's the case, we'll have to rely on conscious memory retention and reinterpretation."

"His heartbeat is slowing down," said Casorati.

"Markedly?"

"It's noticeable. It's a slow, steady decrease."

"Understandable," said Ravelvent. "He's no longer active."

"No," said the doctor. "There's more involved than that. I'm afraid he may be slipping into coma."

"Not with this kind of brain activity," said Ulicon.

"I think the pons may be working rather *too* well," Casorati said. "The decoupling is too effective. His body is losing the rhythm of its continuity. It's as though he were changing metabolic gear. I don't think we dare let this go on too long."

"I don't want to interfere unless I have to," said Ulicon. "It's bound to affect retention and the coherency of the experience if I try and break it up."

"That's a risk you'll have to take," replied Casorati. "I can give you a couple more minutes. That's all."

"It's all right," said Ulicon, quickly. "I think the decline is having a feedback effect. Look!"

The oscillograph trace changed its character rapidly, the ever-changing pulse giving way to a rhythmic, high-amplitude, low-frequency trace that gained stability very quickly.

"It's over," said Ulicon. "Now I'm going to stimulate him just a little, bring him out of the deep sleep, so that he'll hear what I'm saying, and be able to reply."

"Not so fast," said Casorati, reaching out a hand to make Ulicon pause. But Ulicon pushed the doctor's arm away.

"It has to be now," he said. "While the experience is still accessible."

On the oscillograph, the frequency of the wave increased, and the amplitude began to vary slightly.

Joth's mouth opened—as far as the complex web of apparatus around his head would permit it to open—and a thin sound between a moan and a sigh escaped from his lips.

"Joth," said Ulicon, careful to pronounce his words clearly, "can you hear me?"

They waited.

33.

The voice filled Joth's internal cosmos. There was nothing else. Except for his hearing, his sensory apparatus was disengaged and disinterested. He was in the mental limbo which results from the complete relaxation of the higher faculties. The voice was an invasion. It came to him not *via* the vibration of the tympanum, but by electronic stimulation of the auditory receptors in the brain, *via* the artificial ears of the medical cyborg of which Joth was a part.

Joth did not respond.

But the voice came again, cutting into his state of relaxation, disturbing the limbo of his mind. It would not let his consciousness rest, but forced it into a state of minimum reactivity.

From the words, he read the meaning, and he organized an answer. The process by which he did so was largely automatic, involving no actual cogitation.

"I hear you," said his mind. The voice picked up the words, and they came out in a low murmur.

"Joth." The words came at him again. "Joth, did you make contact?"

He sorted the meaning from the words, but did not react.

("I'll have to ask more specific questions," said Ulicon to his companions, his hand covering the microphone. "I'll have to lead him. He can only answer literally—I can't leave too much unsaid, because he simply won't be able to supply the extra meaning.")

"Joth," said the voice, "you have been dreaming. When your dream was ending, you saw something, didn't you? What did you see?"

And Joth replied: "I saw Camlak."

A pause. Then the voice said: "Did you talk to Camlak?"

"I talked to Camlak," replied Joth.

"Where is Camlak?"

Joth hesitated. Words trembled on his lips, but all that finally formed was: "Camlak is...."

"Is he in the Underworld?"

No answer. Ulicon amended the question: "Is Camlak in the Underworld?"

Still confusion. Still searching for words. Finally, Joth said: "Camlak is inside elsewhere."

"I want you to tell me what Camlak said to you," said the voice. "What did Camlak say to you?"

(Ulicon licked his lips. This was the crucial question. If Joth could answer this—and if his answer made sense—then here was the only possible direct access to what Joth might have learned. If this did not work, then he would have to rely on Joth's interpretative mind to try and recover the essence of the experience. If it could.)

Joth spoke:

"Soul space," he said. "Child two. One and one. Link chain. Change mind. All soul. Child shadow. Shape wall. Flow I all. Soul through. Hillsunfireli...shi...see...flo...o...."

Joth's voice died into an incoherent mumble, where the sounds crumbled together and would not make words.

("It's gibberish," said Clea Aron.

"No," said Ulicon. It's the vocal component of the communication—so far as it can be approximated. Where it breaks down it does so because that's where the vocal component of the exchange broke down. The substance of the contact must have been imagistic, with verbal support...mind to mind, direct telepathic communication with a minimum of translatory mediation. What we have is the verbal core of the message. That's what we wanted. If only Joth can build on that. When he returns to full consciousness, his mind is going to try and integrate the message into his awareness of existence—it may fail or succeed incompletely. The ideas may become changed, or may even be erased. But we have the core as it is. We have something to work with."

"For what it's worth," added Ravelvent. "Some of those two-word units could mean any of a hundred different things."

"But Joth can help us," said Ulicon, "if only his mind can retain enough of the experience.")

The voice was still. Everything was still. Joth floated in limbo, inactive, unaware, for a timeless interval....

...And then began the coalescence of consciousness which would bring him back to the reified world, and secure him within the cage of solid reality.

34.

The broadcast which was intended to capture the world and secure the new government required only three people. Plus, of course, the technology and the technical staff required to package the message and see it safely into every home in every continent. The three people were to play three archetypal roles, and between them, they were to define the synthetic product which, following the end of the broadcast would define the "way of life" in which the citizens of the Overworld were to be participants. The purpose of the broadcast was, quite simply, to redefine the entire context of life: to rationalize the change, not of circumstance, but of intellectual ecology, which had become necessary. The revolutionaries set out, in fact, to rewrite the entire mental environment of Euchronia's citizens, so that they would no longer *be* Euchronia's citizens.

The achievement of this purpose would be by no means easy, but it was a practical aim requiring a relatively simple method. The people of the Overworld were parasitic upon the machine complex which supplied them with all the necessities and luxuries of life. They had no option but to be defined by the machine. It is a principle of evolutionary inevitability that parasites, in becoming adapted to their hosts, lose their organs of locomotion, their sense organs, and everything which extends them beyond themselves: they cease to be whole organisms, and become part-organisms. When the host is redefined, so is the parasite. The people of the Overworld contained relatively little of their whole existence within their individual minds—most of it was contained by the cybernet. As the nature of the information carried by the cybernet changed therefore—as the holovisual network began to "think different thoughts"—so the nature of Euchronia's citizens was made to change. The people themselves began to think different thoughts. The change was not easy—there was confusion, emotional disturbance and insecurity—but it was inevitable.

The first of the three people involved in the renaissance of the Overworld was Yvon Emerich. He represented the people—he was their representative within the "thoughts" of the cybernet. (The reference here, of course, is to the projected image of Emerich rather than to the real individual—it was the image with which people were invited to identify.) It was Emerich's task to "present" the program, to organize it and provide the ideas which were to be contained in it with a human context, a human environment. He was to be aggressive, but not destructive, rhetorical but not informative.

The second of the three was Eliot Rypeck. His job was to define the problem. It was up to him to destroy the old patterns of thought, to expose ruthlessly the error and the hopelessness of the old regime. He represented the problem, building an edifice of fear and naked truth, defining a fire-breathing dragon to threaten the world.

The third man required by the scheme was, of course, the hero—a new figurehead. He was not required to do anything at all, but simply to *be*. He (the image, not the man) would become the new focus of hope, the new organizing principle within the mechanical mind of the Overworld. His name, of course, was Joel Dayling.

35.

"What happened to Camlak," said Joth, "wasn't simply a translocation. He...twisted himself...out of our space into another but there was more to it than that. In a way, it was also a metamorphosis, a transfiguration. Camlak now is not the same kind of being that he was. He has *transcended* that whole mode of being, and now he is something new. He retains aspects of himself, and it is through these aspects that he was able to make contact with me, and to transfer ideas from his mind into mine. But there's more to it than that...more that is beyond our understanding. I can't explain because there is no explanation. It is outside what we know and understand."

"I want you to go over the things which you said while you were still unconscious," said Ulicon. "Expand on them any way you can. We don't want exact explanations—we simply want to know the contexts in which the words are to be set."

"All right," said Joth. "One by one. Give them to me."

"Soul space," said Ulicon.

"That's what I've just been trying to tell you about," said Joth. "There are other spaces, outside, or perhaps alongside, this one. But the space where Camlak is is not only apart from ours—it's intrinsically *different* from it. There seems to be less fixity in it, the reality is less *solid*, less unitary. It's as though several possibilities may exist simultaneously...except that there's no simultaneity...go on to the next."

Ravelvent obviously wanted to interrupt, to ask for clarification, but Ulicon signaled him to be still.

"Child two," he said.

"That's simple," said Joth. "It simply means that the Children of the Voice are two beings in one. They have a human-like aspect, but they also have a Gray Soul—they aren't individuals."

"One and one," read Ulicon.

"The same point. Meant to convey, I think, some kind of equality of the creature which we see and understand, and the

Soul. We mustn't think of the Soul as being 'in' the person—there is simply a touching point between them: an interface, not in the brain, but in the mind."

"You're making a clear distinction between the two?" asked Ulicon.

"I think we have to."

"Very well. Link chain."

Joth considered for a moment. "I think this refers to the fact that the nature of the relationship between the Children of the Voice and their Gray Souls, the potential exists for the linking of minds in some kind of linear fashion. I can't quite see how."

"What about 'Change mind'?"

"Just what it says, I think. Minds can be changed—they have the power of metamorphosis, though I don't know how or why. The act itself seems rather self-evident, but I think I that's all there is."

"All Soul."

This time, Joth paused for a long time before answering. "All I can make of that," he said, finally, "is that we can all become like the Souls. But that may simply be a rationalization of the statement itself. I don't remember anything in connection with the phrase."

"Child shadow."

Joth shook his head. "I think I'm losing it," he said. "These things must have meant something *then*—during the contact. But I've lost the meaning now. It seems to me to suggest that the Children of the Voice are in some sense shadows—perhaps from the viewpoint of the Souls. There's an old saying—something about our world, as we see it, being only the shadows of reality...perhaps that's the perspective the phrase is intended to convey."

Ulicon nodded. "I think you may be right. The next phrase is 'Shape wall', which seems to tie in."

"It may," said Joth. "We are merely the shapes on the wall—the shadows cast by the firelight. I think that's right—it's just an image, to help us think."

"There are two syllables in the final jumble of words," said Ulicon. "After 'hill' and 'sun' you said 'fireli.' That may be the beginning of 'firelight.' And at that point the verbal thinking seems to be giving way to visual imagery. 'Shi,' which came next, might be the beginning of 'shining.' But there are two more distinct phrases yet. The first is 'Flow all.'"

Joth rubbed his eyes, and tensed the muscles of his face as though to force reluctant ideas into his head. "It could mean so many things," he said. "I have no intuition...I honestly think that at this stage I'm no more competent to interpret than you are. It might mean that in the other space everything can flow... nothing is fixed. But it may mean something else entirely. It's just gone from my mind. There's nothing there to echo."

"Try the last," said Ulicon, kindly. "Soul through."

Joth was shaking his head even as the words were spoken.

"Nothing," he said. "It means nothing. The only thing I can think of is that the Souls can come through into our space just as Camlak went into theirs...no, I'm sure that's not it. It's something else. But something I can't reach...."

"Relax," said Ulicon. "There's no hurry. It may come to you some other time—it may even come back to you in your dreams. You've done magnificently—far better than we could have hoped. You established contact, and you brought something back from the contact. Perhaps we can't understand, but we know that we're on the way to understanding. We've brought this thing into the realm of things we can *study*, things we can work with. We may not know what we're doing, but we can begin to feel our way."

"It's dangerous," said Ravelvent, no longer able to contain his impatience. "You seem to have become so wrapped up in this that you've forgotten that we're playing with forces that could destroy the world."

"We already have those," retorted Ulicon, calmly. "We've been living with atomic power for millennia. To an extent, we run the world on forces which—if we couldn't control them— could destroy it. Such forces exist, and we can't pretend we live in a world without them." He paused to glance at his wristwatch. "And now, I think we must return to the real world. We've exempted ourselves for a considerable time, in order to conduct this experiment. If you, Joachim, would activate the holovid, I think we can listen to what Eliot has to say."

He looked round at the expressions of startled puzzlement.

"There's no need to be alarmed," he assured them. "The world simply has a new messiah. Like all the others, he's only going to promise to save us from ourselves."

36.

"The objectives of the Euchronian Movement," Rypeck was saying, "were both clear and narrow. They were products of the age that we now call the age of psychosis, or the Second Dark Age. In earlier periods of history there had been no clear and narrow objectives adopted and accepted by any substantial and cosmopolitan body of men. This is not to say that individuals lacked any sense of purpose, but that the race as a whole lacked any unified concept of historical ambition. The Euchronian Movement set forth a system of priorities which, for the first time, provided a focus for the whole of mankind.

"We still live with the objectives and priorities of the Movement of eleven thousand years ago. We have the world that they designed. In order to build the world we now inhabit, the Movement changed mankind. The Movement *became* mankind, first of all, by so defining itself—the men who would not accept commitment to the Movement's ends were abandoned, and left to die on the surface, entombed by the platform.

"But that was not enough. Mankind had to be changed in order that the Movement's evaluation of itself should be justified. The Movement had defined the destiny of man—plotted his future history. It had designed the world he must live in, and prescribed total commitment to the Plan as the only means of achieving that world-vision. Having defined the Plan as the perfect statement of human need, it proceeded to adapt mankind to the Plan. Having defined clear and simple objectives, the Movement set out to manufacture a clear and simple human race.

"One of the instruments which the Movement found in order to further this end—to protect the Plan against human weakness—was a drug known as the i-minus agent. This drug was administered to the builders in both food and water. Its purpose was to eliminate the instinctive element in human nature, to make men more pliable, more easily indoctrinated—to make them, in fact, better servants of the Plan. This was done in secret, and the secret entrusted to a handful of men—not even to the whole Council of the Movement.

"That drug is still being administered today. The motives behind the i-minus project were good. The Movement saw the Plan as the only hope for humanity, and human nature as the only threat to the Plan. In attempting to enslave humanity to their particular set of ideals they were—by their own definition—'right.' And in some measure, they succeeded in enslaving mankind to their particular set of ideals. We still hold, for the most part, to the set of values established by the planners. Such dissent as there is among us is not due to the instinctive, animal qualities which the Movement sought to exorcise, but to variance in what we learn, what we think, and what we come to believe.

"But it is surely time, now, to ask questions about this drug, and what it has made of us. Such questions have always been asked, but they have been asked and answered in secret, debated by a handful of individuals. While this has been going on, our world has come to the brink of disaster. It is my conviction that part of the reason why we seem so completely helpless in the face of our present circumstances is the work of the i-minus agent. We have been fitted to the well-defined and narrow concept of what a human being should be, as decided by the Euchronian Movement. But the problems we face at this time are not problems which—according to Euchronian philosophy—human beings ought to face. In defining man as they did, the Euchronian Movement also defined the world in which he existed. We have discovered that the world is simply not like that.

"We live in the Overworld designed by the Planners. But the Planners saw the Overworld as the *whole* world, the limits of existence. Outside the walls of Utopia, there is supposedly nothing. If the vast universe of the stars exists, then it is somehow apart from human life: quintessential. If the world within—the Underworld—exists, then that, too, is apart from human life and completely irrelevant to it.

"We have found that this is not so. Outside the walls of Utopia, the world goes on. We have found that the Universe is real, that the stars have worlds and peoples. We have contrived to ignore that, despite the fact that had it not been for the people of another world the Plan could not have been brought to its conclusion in the manner that it was. We also contrived to ignore the Underworld, doubting its reality, for thousands of years. But now we can no longer ignore it. We can no longer retain even the illusion of our total isolation from anything beyond the machine in which we live. We have been invaded—we *can* be invaded. We have reacted to the first of these, but it is really the second which concerns us.

"The fact is very simply that we have been wrong. The Movement defined humanity and human life too narrowly. In trying to shape man to the mold which it made for him, the Movement robbed him of an adaptability which may have prevented our ever reaching the predicament in which we now find ourselves. Of all the people on the platform, only one— the alien, Sisyr—remembered the Underworld. Had there been more—if the Planners, too, had remembered—then the terrible shock of confrontation which we have suffered could not have happened.

"The aims of the Movement were a response to the situation of the Second Dark Age. They were designed to end that Second Dark Age and prevent any such age of psychosis from recurring. Now, we need a new set of priorities—a new prescription for action—which is a response to our present circumstances. Rafael Heres reacted to what has happened in the manner of a man totally committed to the ideas which are now out of date. His only answer was to destroy—to fulfill the assumptions which had proved unjustified by destroying the proof. It was his belief that the Overworld was the *whole* world, and he attempted to confirm that belief by destroying everything else. At first, he wanted to make the Underworld an extension of the Overworld—to convert it into a human world for human beings. When he found that that was simply not possible, he found no other alternative but to exterminate all life within it, to render it inert.

"But even if that were possible, it would not be an answer. We know now what we ought to have known all the time—that the Overworld is not all that exists. It is not the whole Earth, and it is certainly not the whole Universe.

"It is we who must change. It is we who must adapt to what we know, rather than wasting ourselves in the futile attempt to adapt what really exists to our narrow concept of existence.

"We should be grateful for the fact that this revelation has been forced upon us now, and that we did not endure in our state of willful ignorance for a few centuries more. If we had continued as we were, the realization that the Overworld is not inviolable would have come to us in a manner even more frightening than the way in which it has.

"The pillars which support the platform—the structures which hold up our world—have been corroded and weakened. At the present, there seems to be little danger of imminent collapse, but it is clear that the supporting structure not only needs rapid repair, but constant attention thereafter. If we had not been forced to look into the world beneath our feet we would not have discovered this until it was too late.

"We must, therefore, in order to maintain our existence, go back into the Underworld—not as invaders or exterminators of vermin, but as workers and builders. We will be forced to come to terms with the Underworld and its peoples, and those terms cannot and must not be the terms of total war, because our total war is a failure.

"The reactivity of the life-system in the Underworld is such that the viruses with which we sought to destroy it are by no means effective. If all that we had to do was kill, perhaps, in a very long time, we might succeed in wiping out the life of the Underworld. But we have much more to think about than killing. We have to think about repairing the pillars—*all* the pillars, in all quarters of the globe. The work that needs to be done is tremendous, and it will require a concerted effort on the part of our society. We cannot do this work if we are simultaneously to wage an all-out global war with the Underworld. Rather, we need to make peace with the people of the Underworld, to cooperate with them, and—if possible—to enlist their help. This will not be easy, and in some respects it may be as difficult as our attempt to wage war, but this is what needs to be done if we are to adapt ourselves to reality. We must come to understand the people of the Underworld, and find a means of coexisting with them. We must cease to think of them as 'the men on the ground'—Euchronia's enemies— because they are something different, something new. Carl Magner tried to tell us that we must show the Face of Heaven to the people of the Underworld, because we were wrong to deny them the sight of it. I think that we must also show *ourselves* the Face of Heaven, because we have been wrong to refuse to look at it."

37.

It was not until Rypeck was replaced by Dayling that Ulicon's companions fully understood what had happened. Clea Aron had known what would happen, in an approximate sense, but she had not been involved in any way with the transfer of authority—she had merely agreed to remain passive. Ravelvent was not surprised by the turn taken by events, although he was somewhat startled by the apparent smoothness of the operation, which had happened virtually while his back was turned.

Casorati was the only one who expressed his surprise:

"You *knew* this was happening!" he said to Ulicon.

Ulicon nodded. "I think it was well done," he said. "Eliot was perfect. Long-winded and dry, but casual and rhetorical. Then Dayling, to repeat the same message in brief, emotional tones."

"And that's it?" asked Clea Aron. "That's going to change the world, overnight."

"Oh yes," said Ulicon. "You shouldn't assume that because the Movement held total control for thousands of years, and claimed absolute stability, that it can't be set aside. Its very constancy has led to its being taken wholly for granted. The people had simply become unconscious of government—so far as their everyday lives are concerned the machine rules, and the mind behind it is totally invisible. They'll accept the change. All, perhaps, except the hierarchy of the Movement, many of whom will find themselves out of a job. But it's only political positions that will be affected —the civil services will simply carry on. I doubt if there will be any more unrest in the world tonight than there was last night—perhaps less, now that the people have some new hope of order being recovered out of the confusion."

"But you just carried on with the experiment," said Casorati, as though he was almost unable to conceive of it.

"The experiment was important," said Ulicon. "More important, perhaps, than what was happening out there."

"It won't work," said Ravelvent. "The new program is as helpless as the old in dealing with the one thing which really matters—the fact that the people are desperately afraid of a recurrence of the mental invasion."

"There will be no recurrence," said Ulicon.

"Why not?"

"Because the i-minus project is finished. The i-minus agent which, we have reason to believe, enabled the event to take place and—perhaps more important—helped render people vulnerable to the event when it did. The cessation of the project will minimize the effect of the telepathic input, and may even stop it altogether."

"You don't know," said Ravelvent. "You don't know that at all. This experiment isn't proof of that theory, isn't even evidence for it."

"We will act upon the assumption that we are right," said Ulicon. "We will promise the people that there will be no recurrence of the blast. We won't tell them that everything will be wonderful—the recovery of the instinctive input into the psyche isn't going to be easy. But what we are doing—what we will say that we are doing—is readapting them to the world. They will accept what we say, unless there is another blast to prove us wrong."

"And if there is?"

"Then what can anyone do? What solution could there be? We can only act upon the assumption that we will survive. If there is another mindblast, if our minds are taken apart and destroyed, then that spells the end. Adapting to *that* would be far beyond the scope of political action. We must assume that we will win, and we will assure the people that we *know* we will win. And we will hope that we are telling the truth. Only time will tell."

Clea Aron pointed at the image of Joel Dayling on the screen.

"Do you honestly think that *he* is any better than Heres?" she asked.

They all turned to look at the new Hegemon. He was winding up his own version of what Rypeck had said, speaking in clipped sentences, with convinced sincerity and carefully practiced self-assurance.

"No," said Ulicon. "Not if you mean 'Do I think he is a better man.' In many ways, Rafe and he are alike. But that's not what matters. What matters is the fact that he can organize some kind of social action which will help to get us out of this mess, whereas Heres no longer could. Heres had worked himself into a blind corner. A trap. A new figurehead was desperately needed.

Rypeck tried to persuade Acheron Spiro, before the emergency arose, but Spiro couldn't have taken Heres' place. Not as we are now. It needed someone new, someone from outside. Dayling is all we had."

"A Eupsychian."

Ulicon shrugged. "That doesn't matter either. The changes which will happen now will render the conflict between Euchronia and its Eupsychian rebels quite meaningless."

"I think you overestimate the power we have to change ourselves," said Ravelvent. "I don't think that Dayling and his party—whoever his party are—will be able to organize society along the lines you suggest. I think we may well see a breakup of central organization. I think you'll see other leaders emerging, and—more important—you'll see mass resignation from the social order. People will simply quit."

"We control the cybernet," said Ulicon. "And while we control the cybernet we control *everything*. Not only what people do, but what they think and what they are. Your thinking is thousands of years out of date, Abram. Certainly, they'll opt out. Tomorrow morning, they'll be flocking to the sanctuaries. But they won't stay there. How can they? The sanctuaries depend on the cybernet for their existence just as everything else does. In a matter of months, the sanctuaries will be back to their normal transient population, and the people will be working under the new regime, according to its ministrations."

"And anyone who objects, no doubt, will be working in the Underworld." This piece of sarcasm was contributed by Casorati. Ulicon did not favor him with a reply.

"At least," said Joth—the first words he had spoken since he had heard Rypeck tell the world that the Underworld had to be saved rather than destroyed—"we are returning to sanity."

"If we can find it," said Ravelvent.

38.

Iorga knelt to drink water from the shallow pool surrounded by blocks of cracked cement. The blocks were encrusted with red and yellow lichenous growths, and the water was thick with monads and thin filaments of algae. Huldi threw herself full-length on the ground, leaning over the lip of the pool to splash water into her face.

The region was hot, and the air heavy and humid. Under his clothing, Iorga was sweating copiously, and both Huldi and Nita were flushed—almost feverish. They were in a clear area, relatively speaking. The buildings forming the framework of the forest were gigantic, but they were well-spaced. In between them, the plants clung to other structures, but none more than a man's height. Iorga felt very small as he contemplated the vast blocks which reached high into the sky—so high that their roofs seemed almost to touch the stars.

These reinforced concrete monsters had—in the old world—been faced with glass, but that was all gone now. Only the skeletons remained.

The life-system had moved into the buildings as well as dressing their exterior walls, and inside each of the structures there would be great communities of organisms on every floor. Every building was a multilayered concrete island.

Iorga's ears pricked, searching the damp air for any vestige of vibration. His eyes searched the mottled carpet of fungus. His nose told him that something was wrong, but he searched with his other senses for some kind of confirmation.

All he could see and hear were the great ghost-moths fluttering around the towers where they swarmed. The unsteady flickering of their vast white wings caught the light and reflected it with a curious stroboscopic effect which constantly drew his eyes only to mislead them. The thin screeching of the moths, in the highest register of his hearing, filled his ears, and any more subtle, lower pitched sounds were lost. Smaller insects, silent in flight, with jeweled, transparent wings, mingled with the ghost-moths in their aerial dance. Some of them were stinging wasps, but they did not seem alarmed by the presence of the three invaders.

Iorga climbed a low ridge of basidiomycetic fiber, attempting to command a better view of the surroundings, but it would not bear his weight. In supporting himself with his hand he found that the vegetable tissue was rotten inside, swarming with maggots. As he held up his hand to inspect the putrefying gel which stuck to it, flies began to gather around it. He shook off the gel and wiped the moisture from his palm.

Nita, seeing the suspicion in his attitude, sniffed the air carefully.

"Fire," she commented.

"Cuchumanates," said Iorga. "They came through the blight ahead of us. These lands are their lands if they are anyone's. They may attack."

The doubt in his mind was clear in his voice. The Cuchumanates were dangerously unpredictable. If they did attack, the fight would be savage—it would be no mere skirmish.

The safest thing by far was to keep well clear. But the heat did not make traveling easy.

Huldi caught a hopping insect with a swift movement of her hand, bit into the abdomen, and sucked out the soft part of the creature, then threw the chitinous shell away.

"Eat," she said. "While we can."

"There!" said Iorga, suddenly, pointing west—the direction they wanted to go. When Nita followed the direction of his arm, she could see nothing, but she knew that the hellkin had detected movement.

"This way," said Iorga, reaching down to haul Huldi to her feet. With his head, he indicated that they were to move to the right, into the shadow of one of the monstrous frameworks. Huldi gathered together the food and the weapon she had been carrying, and they all ran across the open space to the overgrown wall.

As they reached its shelter, an arrow struck the plant flesh above the hellkin's head, and sank into it with a dull, liquid sound.

Pushing the others before him, Iorga retreated along the wall. He saw one of the Cuchumanates coming forward at a run, then another. There was no longer any question of hiding—they must escape or kill.

They found an opening in the wall—what had once been a considerable doorway but which was now reduced to a narrow, oval aperture.

"Inside," said Iorga. Nita went through immediately, but Huldi was reluctant. To her, the interior seemed pitch-black, and she had a horror of closed, dark spaces which were certain to be full of biting insects. Her eyes were not so sharp as those possessed by Nita, let alone the cat-eyes of the hellkin. Iorga had to go ahead of her, and then pull her in after him.

Nita found the corridor within much wider and taller than the entrance had suggested, but strands of webbing were everywhere. She had to pull the thin, slightly sticky strands away from her face. She could see little save the broad dimensions of the place, but she could hear multifold rustling noises as the denizens of the hall retreated from the intrusion.

Iorga drew the gun— it was a pistol—that Joth had left with him on his return to the Overworld. Huldi also held a weapon at the ready—a long, stout knife of Heaven-sent metal, but Nita's best knife was made of bone. Iorga considered giving up his own metal knife, but decided against it.

He had only a limited quantity of ammunition for the pistol, and when it was empty...it made sense to let the biggest and strongest handle the most effective weaponry.

The hellkin crouched in the doorway, looking out. The Cuchumanates had decided that caution was required, and they were approaching slowly, hidden by the tangled maze of puff-balls and toadstools.

While he waited, Huldi crouched by his side, crowding him,

determined not to move back from the entrance and the weak light of the road of stars.

Another arrow scored the collar of fungus round the aperture, harmlessly dislodging a piece of rind and carrying it ten or twelve feet into the maw of the cave.

Then one of the attackers came to her feet and ran forward, bone-tipped spear clutched in both hands and extended before her. Iorga had time to look at the thin face, the skin stretched like tanned pigskin over the sharp cheekbones. He saw the crazy anger in the bloodshot eyes.

She was no more than five strides away when he fired.

She had been running forward at a good pace, and she was big and raw-boned, but the bullet nevertheless picked her up off her feet and threw her backwards. It struck below the rib cage, just above the navel, and its flat trajectory carried it clean through her body, blasting out half her gut through the exit hole. As she hit the ground she writhed, as if trying to bounce back to her feet, and though she could not, her arms continued to grope for support. Her convulsive movement broke the soft haft of the spear in two.

Had Iorga been facing the Men Without Souls or his own kind—perhaps even a pack of harrowhounds, that might have been the end of the battle. The others would have run. But the Cuchumanates, more even than the Ahrima, did not withdraw once they were committed.

Two arrows flew into the aperture, missing both Iorga and Huldi, who made as much use of the cover as possible. One nicked Nita's clothing as it went past, and drew blood from a scratch on her arm. Although she was not hurt, the shock of the impact made her draw back, moving sideways to the wall of the corridor, where she pressed her body up against the rusts and the masks. She felt something crawling in her hair, and picked it away with her fingernails, cracking its exoskeleton as she threw it aside.

Iorga fired again, and missed.

Two of the attackers were coming at him, and though he was

careful to let them come far enough so that he ought not to waste bullets, his aim was not good enough. The pistol was a little unsteady in his fist. As the point of a spear jabbed at his face, he recoiled from the doorway, cocking the gun again. The narrowness of the opening saved him, as the Cuchumanates got in one another's way trying to come through. Huldi thrust at one, and gashed her leg, while Iorga's third shot tore a black hole in the other's left eye. Again, the momentum of the bullet carried the body backwards, and the second attacker was bowled over. Because of the wound pouring blood from her leg she was slow to rise, and Iorga had no difficulty in putting a bullet into her.

Huldi expected more of the Cuchumanates to be crowding the doorway within seconds, but there were none. Iorga leaned forward to see better, but only one of the attackers was visible, half-hidden by a swollen dendrite. She was notching an arrow to the string of her bow. Iorga dared not fire, because she was too far away for him to be sure of hitting her.

Nita shouted a wordless warning, and he whirled, to see three or four shadows moving from a distant corner. He fired at them, and they parted as though to let the missile through. He heard it hit a wall behind them and whine as it ricocheted. Realizing that the Cuchumanates knew of—or had discovered—another way in, Iorga moved back, away from the dimly lit aperture.

"This way," he hissed, and moved off diagonally across the hallway, toward the darkness where there were other doors. As he heard the Cuchumanates coming at him he sprinted. Nita scuttled alongside him.

Huldi, meanwhile, could not simply launch out into the blackness. She could not see the darker shadows for which the others were headed. Instead of following directly, she moved along the wall, feeling her way with one hand while the other waved the metal knife in slow horizontal arcs. She felt blind terror, knowing that the Cuchumanates must be able to see her even though she could not see them. But nothing came near to her blade, and nothing ripped at her throat.

Iorga stumbled, and pitched forward onto a ridged slope—a

staircase. He took the skin off the knuckles of his gun hand, but did not lose his grip on the weapon. He started up the stair, with Nita following. After ten or twelve steps he whirled round to look back. The Cuchumanates were well-nigh at the girl's heels. Steadying his right wrist with his left hand he fired over Nita's shoulder, once, twice and again. Then the gun was empty, but the Cuchumanates were gone. One was crumpled at the foot of the stairs, screaming in agony, the others had leapt backwards, retreating behind the corners of the opening at the foot of the stairs.

Iorga pushed Nita, indicating that she must go on upwards. He took advantage of the momentary respite to empty the spent cartridges from the gun and fit a fresh clip. Then he followed, backing up the steps one by one.

Meanwhile, Huldi had come to a corner and rounded it, and was still moving along, her hand guiding her by touching the wall. She heard a sound, and was sure that at least one of the Cuchumanates was now coming after her. She began to run.

Then the wall which half-supported her was suddenly no longer there. In reaching to find it she overbalanced, and fell into a yawning, invisible opening.

Vomit rose into her mouth as she fell, and there was just time to wonder if she would shatter her bones before she smashed into a concrete floor and lost consciousness.

39.

The helicopter settled on the flat area at the western edge of the roof of Sisyr's house. The alien eased himself out of the safety harness and climbed down, ducking away from the fierce airflow stirred up by the decelerating blades.

The whine of the blades decreased in pitch as he moved away. The police captain followed him out, and then stood for a few moments, waiting until the noise had died down sufficiently for him to speak in a normal tone.

"The men who were in your house have all reported back in," he said. "They were told to leave everything as they found it. If there's any damage, anything missing, let us know. I'm afraid that there's bound to have been some degree of disturbance. If you need any help...."

"There is no need," said the alien. "I have all the time I need."

The official looked uncertain for a few seconds, as though he felt that he ought to say something more, but he decided, instead, to retreat from the situation and let Sisyr fade away into his forgotten corner of the Earth. He raised his hand in an odd mock salute, and then clambered back up into the belly of the helicopter.

The rotor blades were still whirling. The moment the captain was back inside, they began to pick up speed again and the whine began again.

Sisyr moved back, and then watched the helicopter dance away into the sky, swinging round to head away into a bank of dull gray cloud that was moving in from the north. The alien waited awhile, seeing the snowclouds filling half the sky, and then three-quarters. The first thick flakes were tumbling out of the sky, settling in his clothing, before he finally turned away and walked slowly to the door.

Sisyr's house was very large by the standards of Euchronia. Through well hidden in the higher slopes of a mountain range, with the towering islands of the old surface all around, it was an imposing sight when glimpsed from the flat platform plain below. It suited its ancient surroundings, like an ancient castle or palace.

For the most part, the houses used by Euchronia's citizens were small, rarely accommodating more than a handful of people. There was no reason why a citizen of Euchronia should not have as much space as he required, but the acquisitive habits of the prehistoric ages had not, for the most part, been recovered by the people of the new world. There were many collectors in Euchronia, but they tended to be selective and discriminating. The old compulsion to accumulate for the sake of accumulation, so common among the prehistoric leisured classes, had been one of the things frowned upon by the Movement in its earliest days.

Sisyr, however, had provided for himself a vast dwelling with a multitude of rooms. His priorities were rather different from those of mortal men. The scope of his projects and pastimes had to be so much the greater.

He made his way to a room with one wall made completely of glass—a great window positioned so that he could stand by it and see the extent of the mountain slopes on either side of him, and beyond them the great cornfields which stretched for hundreds of miles across the platform, tended only by machines. Today, though, he did not stand, but brought up to the window a high-backed chair. He got food and drink from the cybernet, and he seated himself to take his meal in the shadow of the storm which gathered about his home.

It was not a violent storm, by the standards of the region, but there was some thunder and lightning, and the snow drove hard against the glass wall and tried to stick, to build a curtain of white which would close out the world.

As he finished his meal, he heard someone enter the room by a door behind him. He did not look round, but simply waited. He was aware of the intruder walking across the carpeted floor, to stand just behind the chair.

"I've never seen snow," said a voice. "That's rather strange, isn't it? So much happens in the world that we remain unaware of. For instance, I never knew about the mountains. I suppose, in my brain, I must have stored the fact that some mountain peaks from the old world project beyond the platform, but I really never *thought* about it. It never occurred to me that some of the Underworld is actually above the Overworld. Pieces of the prehistoric past. Is there, perhaps, a lost race of Second Dark Age people lurking somewhere nearby?"

In the glass before him, Sisyr could see a faint reflective image of the man who was speaking. He had seen the man before, if only on a screen. In a sense, this man and he had been involved with one another for a considerable time.

His name was Jervis Burstone.

He was holding a gun.

"I was informed that the police had left," said Sisyr, calmly.

"They did," replied Burstone. "When they left, we came in."

"We?"

"There are a dozen of us. There may be more. We're still making contacts...preparations...."

"Preparations for what?" Sisyr still did not turn. Burstone inched forward, until he was beside the alien, and he made sure that Sisyr could, by the merest sideways glance, see that he held the weapon.

"This is a weird place to build a home," said Burstone. "It's cold and bleak. Or is that more like home, to you, than the temperate zone? Perhaps you come from a cold, bleak world, full of bare rock slopes, with a snowline right down to the sea."

"Perhaps," said Sisyr. He had lived on many worlds.

"And the house," said Burstone. "So many rooms, full of so many things. A museum. All those books...you must have as many as the main depository. All that stone. And, of course, all your plunder from the Underworld. How far into the mountain do your cellars extend?"

"Far enough," said Sisyr.

"What are you?" asked Burstone. "Some kind of custodian, holding the history of Earth's two worlds in trust? I often wondered what I was doing, in the name of the Plan, trading garbage with the Underworlders."

"You did it because you wanted to," said Sisyr. "You felt that you were doing something worthwhile. And you were."

"You tricked us. You made us believe that it was all part of the Plan. You made use of what we believed, of the *need* we had to be doing something for the Plan."

"Is that why you've come?" asked Sisyr. "To confront me with your righteous rage? To gain your revenge? Because you're frightened, as you've never been frightened before?"

"I'm not frightened," said Burstone. "I've been into the

Underworld fifty times and more. I'm not afraid of it."

"Of course," said Sisyr.

But Burstone was afraid of the Underworld. Part of the reason why he went back, again and again, was because he was afraid. He fed on fear—it was almost a kind of pleasure. But from the Underworld, there had always been a return—a return into the utter safety and security of the Overworld. In a sense, Burstone was a man who had spent his life in a ritual parody of return to the womb: the mechanical womb of the host cyber-complex. But now the fear upon which he had fed was feeding on him. The Underworld was threatening to invade his womb. And Burstone had found a gun to hide behind. He had found someone to blame.

Still Sisyr watched the blizzard beyond the window. Burstone moved round still further, until his back was pressed up against the glass wall and he could look at Sisyr's blue eyes.

"You helped the people of the Underworld," he said. "You kept them alive. And now they're going to destroy us."

"I didn't keep them alive," said Sisyr. "I kept them self-aware. I preserved some measure of humanity, not only in the men, but in the others. I helped them keep communication and some degree of civilization. I helped to smooth the path of change, to give them some small degree of *control* over that change. At the pace of evolution with which they live, you see, they could so easily have lost everything, and had to start all over again, without really becoming anything new. I wanted to give them the chance of becoming something new—of making use of the tachytelic evolution without falling prey to its demands. But that was the Plan."

"Your Plan."

"If you choose to believe that, you will. But the Plan was neither wholly mine, nor wholly the Euchronians'. At least in part, it was the Plan of the men on the ground. Without some degree of assistance from men on the ground, the platform could not have been built. Surely you realize that."

"It's not true," said Burstone, flatly.

"It doesn't matter," said Sisyr, after a pause. Burstone could almost imagine the sigh which might have preceded the remark, if Sisyr had been human.

"No," said Burstone. "Not any more."

"Why have you come here?" asked the alien.

"We want your help," replied the human.

"Everyone wants my help," said Sisyr. "For more than a hundred years, I have hardly spoken to a human being. And now, all of a sudden, they are flocking to my door, asking for help. I will do all that I can. I have promised you this again and again. But what you want is always something different. You always want the help that I cannot give, and you always want it with a gun in your hand."

"We *need* your help. We must have it. We're prepared to do what we must in order to get it."

"What help?" asked Sisyr. For the first time, he moved. His head bowed, as though he had suddenly become too weary to support it. His spidery hands clenched beneath his chin.

"We want the starship," said Burstone.

40.

Iorga backed up the staircase slowly. No one came after him. That frightened him, because he knew that the Cuchumanates would not give up. If they were not following him, that almost certainly indicated that they knew another way up.

He knew that he and Nita, at least, were trapped. Unless they killed all their enemies, they would not be able to get out of the building. If the Cuchumanates were so inclined, they could simply wait. But that was not the way of the Cuchumanates. Ahrima might have done that—Men Without Souls certainly would have—but the Cuchumanates would make every effort to find and kill the fugitives.

The best thing to do, he decided, was to gain time—to go upwards. There was every chance that he could separate the attackers, spread them out while they hunted him on ten or a dozen different levels.

He felt Nita touch him on the arm. She was feeling her way. It was so dark now, even to his sensitive eyes, that sight was almost useless.

"Up," he murmured. "Keep going."

"Huldi?" she asked.

"I don't know." He hoped that she might, perhaps, have evaded the attackers and got away outside, but it seemed more likely that the Cuchumanates had caught and killed her.

While they continued the ascent, there was a steady susurrus of noise around them as the larger creatures inhabiting the corridor moved away from them. Much of the clicking and faint buzzing came from insects too small to be worrisome, but they both knew only too well that there might be creatures here as dangerous as the Cuchumanates. Nita remembered the coenocytic creatures which had come out of the blackland to destroy the armored vehicles from the Overworld.

Iorga felt Nita suddenly flinch, and she swayed back toward him, her fingers grasping at his clothing. The steps were overgrown, and it was easy to fall, so he reached out immediately to steady her. When she was safe, he let her guide his hand out to touch the obstruction from which she had recoiled.

The passage was blocked by a soft, warm substance. It had the stickiness of the trailing spiderwebs, but it was solid. It yielded slightly to pressure, like a heavy curtain, but it did not tear. He ran his hand from side to side, and then reached upwards, to confirm that the barrier extended all the way across the corridor.

"Take the left wall," he said to Nita. "I'll take the right. Go down slowly until it opens out."

They descended together, very cautiously, staying level with one another by adjusting to the scraping of each other's hand along the wall. Thus they arrived together at the level beneath the barrier. One way seemed to lead towards dim light—perhaps to the external face where there had once been a window. The other way, Iorga could see nothing.

"This way," he said, pulling Nita to him, and moving toward the distant gleam.

He had spoken in a whisper, but he had betrayed his position nevertheless. He did not know from which direction they came, but they were suddenly upon him—at least two, perhaps more. He felt a knife cutting at his head, though it scraped his shoulder blade and only ripped his clothing, and he felt hands grabbing for his arms, trying to stop him bringing the gun into play.

He swung the gun round, trying to clear space, tracing a full circle at a height which should hit a Cuchumanate's shoulders but miss Nita's head. He collided with one body, but at least one had ducked under the swing, and he felt the blade of a bone weapon sink into his abdomen.

He fired once, and hit the one who had stabbed him. The gun fired without a flash, and still he could see nothing. More hands groped for purchase and fingers fastened on his wrist while he kicked viciously to dislodge someone who had grabbed at his waist. He managed to draw his own knife, and slashed wildly, lefthanded, while he moved rapidly to the side. He grappled desperately with the attacker who was forcing his gun hand outwards, and fired off two shots, without any hope of hitting anything, but trying to startle his assailant into letting go.

Then, for the second time, a blade went into his belly, and this time was driven home hard. It was not a metal blade, but he felt it tearing inside him, and the pain was so intense that he doubled up. With a convulsive jerk he freed his right hand, and drew it in to his body. He fired twice from the hip, at the places where he judged the attackers to be.

He waited for another touch, ready to fire again, but no other touch came. His legs buckled under him, and he fell to the ground. For a moment, he tried to sit up, then he allowed himself to sag until he was resting on the full length of his left side. He drew up his knees, trying to confine the gashes in his belly from which blood was coursing, trying to smother the pain.

A minute passed, and there was no sound save for the buzzing of flies. He was very still. He felt two light touches on his face, then three and four, and he realized that a cloud of small insects was gathering around him. He tried to remember which direction the nearest wall might be, and reached out an explorative hand. His fingers found something soft—the body of one of the Cuchumanates. At his touch, the flesh quivered, but she did not move away, and he guessed that she must be near death. As his fingers explored further, a hand tried to push him away. The hand was hot and wet with blood.

He whispered: "Nita!"

There was no answer.

41.

"You want the starship," echoed Sisyr.

"We want to get away," said Burstone. "We want to go to a new world."

"That's not what you want," said the alien. "And if it were, the starship would be no use to you. No use at all."

"It can take us away from here," insisted Burstone.

Sisyr stared out at the swirling snowflakes for a few moments, and then, abruptly, stood up. Burstone made a defensive gesture with the gun, jerking its barrel up to threaten the alien. But Burstone's hand was shaking. Sisyr strode away from him, toward the keyboard which controlled the input to the house cyberunits.

"Don't touch it," said Burstone.

Sisyr reached out a hand, and tapped the keys with the thin, hard fingers. The window blanked out, becoming a solid face of gray—a screen. Burstone moved away from it.

"Come away!" he commanded.

Sisyr looked over his shoulder at the man with the gun. "On that screen," he said, "I can show you the worlds of your neighbor stars—the worlds that my ship could reach in twenty or fifty of your years. There are only a handful. Wouldn't you like to see? To have a choice of destinations?"

"No."

"No," said Sisyr. "You wouldn't. Because you know, in your mind, that you aren't going anywhere. Humans are not equipped for star travel. The experience would probably kill you, and there is, in any case, nowhere that you could go. Not one star in a million has a planet where you could live. There are a great many such planets, but the distances between them are immense. My starship is not a miracle-machine which defies physics. It cannot travel at the velocity of light—in fact, its acceleration is so slow that it takes many decades even to attain a velocity close to that of light. Once such velocities are reached, subjective time begins to slow down, relative to elapsed time here on Earth and on the planet of destination. But long before then you are old, and the period of deceleration is as long as the period of acceleration. The nearest known world capable of sustaining your kind of life—and mine—is centuries away from here. You could not live to see it. And what if you could? What does an alien world have to offer you that makes it worth going to? What makes it worth all those years of confinement within a tiny metal bubble, sensory starvation and utter loneliness?"

"You tell me," said Burstone.

"I am immortal," said the alien. "To my kind, the centuries do not matter. The distortions of time do not matter. We are equipped, mentally and emotionally, for the interstellar gulfs."

"Then you must make us immortal, too," said Burstone doggedly. "You have the science."

Sisyr shook his head deliberately. "It is not a matter of science," he said. "Do you think that I have some secret elixir of youth? Do you think that the constant renewal of my body is merely a matter of medicine? It is inbuilt. My kind do not age. Our bodies have defense mechanisms which destroy all parasites, all disease. Our faculties of self-repair following physical injury are almost unlimited. If I were cut in two, one part would regenerate—if the cut were precise enough, perhaps both. There is only one way that I am likely to die, and that is by surrendering life—willful death. Perhaps, if every cell were burned—if my ship fell into a star...but these are not likely events.

"You must see that my mind is adapted to these circumstances. Time means very little to me in itself—it is only the rate of experience which is important. During a star-journey I am hardly aware of the passing of time. But your mind is adapted to *your* circumstances. You live at a faster rate, a constant rate. While you are awake, you are the subject of time, not its commander. A star-journey would destroy you, mentally and physically.

"You do not want the starship. Perhaps, for the moment, that is what you imagine. You are afraid, and you feel a desperate need to escape. You feel, because of your fear, that to stay here—to stay anywhere on the Earth—may mean death or the destruction of your mind. But the star-ship is useless. Death, and the destruction of the mind...the very things which you are afraid of...are all that the starship has to offer you. You must know that."

Burstone's composure suddenly broke. He lifted the gun high and brought it's butt crashing down on the back of the chair which Sisyr had vacated. The plastic splintered, and a jagged edge ripped the heel of Burstone's hand. He clutched it to his chest, still clutching the gun. Moments later, he leveled the weapon once again at the alien. There was a small red stain on the front of his tunic.

"Then what *can* we do?" He spat out the words as if they tasted foul in his mouth.

"Wait," said Sisyr. "Whatever happens will happen in any case. There is no way you can exempt yourself. You may die, but it is not something that you can avoid. Sooner or later, you will die anyway. All that has changed, in these last few days, is that you have come to realize how little control you have over the moment of your death. But the change is in you, not in the world. You have never had the power to determine the length of your life, save within the limits permitted by chance and other men. Your fear comes from discovery, not from circumstance.

You must learn to live with what you know."

"You've got to help us!"

"You don't want help," said the alien, quietly. "You demand help which simply does not exist, and you know that. What you want is to avoid responsibility. You want to blame someone for what has happened. You want to pretend that the world has suddenly turned against you, and wants to destroy you, though all that has happened is that you have encountered reality.

"You didn't bring that gun to compel me to give you the starship, or to make me take you to another world. You came here with that gun because you wanted to shoot me, to hurt me, to kill me. You need someone to blame. Rafael Heres wanted exactly the same thing, but he found, in the end, that he couldn't blame me enough. Perhaps you can. I've played a bigger part in your life. It's easier for you, and the others who shared your work. They're waiting for you, aren't they? But what are they waiting to hear? Are they waiting for you to tell them to load their possessions into the starship, and prepare for a great voyage, or are they waiting for you to tell them that you've killed me?"

Sisyr turned his face back to the deck, and his fingers dwelt in the air over the controls, as though hesitating, while he chose between courses of action.

Just as his fingers descended, to begin punching out an instruction, Burstone fired. Three of the bullets hit Sisyr in the back—the rest went wild, smashing into the control deck and setting red warning lights flickering.

As Burstone ran, he saw that the blood pouring from the alien's wounds was brown, like the brown of human skin.

42.

When Nita felt the touch of a Cuchumanate hand on her face, she leaped back from it. In so doing she passed behind Iorga, whose large body sheltered her for a moment.

Had there been more light, she would have stayed to fight, but in the darkness, she had no thought but to get away, to escape. She ran the only way she knew—back up the staircase toward the soft barrier.

As she ran, she heard—or thought she heard—the sound of pursuit. At least one of the attackers, she fancied, was at her heels. When she came to the barrier her knife was already raised to slash the curtain.

The soft substance resisted the bite of the blade for a second or two, then yielded. Once cut, the tissue tore easily, and Nita dragged her blade down in a great arc, then brought it up again to slash sideways, rending the skin of the barrier so that the slit became a yawning hole.

She had no way of knowing how thick the barrier might be, or what lay beyond it, but she had no sooner opened an access when she shoved herself through it. The rubbery tegument through which she had cut was no more than a containing membrane. Beyond it was a loose liquid substance which filled the corridor with foam. It was like walking into a mass of soap bubbles. As she waved her arms before her face, trying to clear a space from which she could breathe, her feet slipped, and she stumbled. The steps were wet, and swarming with vermiform creatures. She fell forward, catching herself on her hands, and the hands, too, crushed the wriggling things. They were several inches long, and three or four in girth, and they were very soft. Wherever her weight fell upon them they burst into liquid slime.

There was air enough in the foam for her to breathe, though it smelled rank, and as she tried to suck it in her mouth filled with the bubble fluid. Its taste was not bitter, but she had to cough to stop the liquid following the air into her lungs. Desperately, she clambered to her feet, and staggered on through the froth, squashing the larvae to death as she did so. Her passage would probably result in the destruction of the whole nest, in any case, as the gaps she had made in the protective membrane would allow predators to come in and feed on the succulent, but helpless, creatures.

Within seconds, she was at the second curtain, and again

her small weapon was already hacking at the air as she reached it. Her movements were frenzied as she pulled and tore a way through and into the corridor beyond, where the air was once more dry and dust-laden. Still coughing, she did not pause for an instant, but continued to scramble her way up the overgrown steps with all possible speed.

Her skin and clothing were wet, her feet and hands be-mired with the soft protoplasm of the crushed larvae. There was not an inch of her skin which did not seem to have been tainted in some way by this colossal organism through whose bowels she ran. All the great building seemed to her to be a single entity—a gigantic corpse in which parasites ran wild. All the worms and the insects and the multitudinous algae and fungi which competed to fill up every chamber, use up every surface, seemed to her akin to the tiny organisms which swarm over every corpse, inside and out, greedy for every last vestige of its decaying substance. And she, with them, felt herself reduced in size to a mere insect, something well-nigh invisible, almost unreal.

Without sight, she could have no real idea of the size and nature of things. There was only touch and smell and hearing, and what these told her was that she was swallowed up by this gigantic creature, that she was one with the cockroaches scrabbling at the walls around her and one with the maggots in their balls of spittle and one with the slithering worms.

Without sight, there was nothing to tell her that she was human.

Living in the moment, as she did, with past and future submerged in the subconscious continuity of her life, she was totally subject to unreasoning panic. Once in the grip of the compulsion to run, to surrender everything in flight, she was completely captive. Her brain ceased to think, and merely let her act.

She was no longer a creature of choice, a thinking being, but only a thing of arms and legs, with a single claw of animal bone.

She drove herself upwards.

Up and up.

A mere handful of compound eyes followed—or tried to follow—the direction of her flight. Most of the creatures who made the staircase—the spinal column of the concrete corpse—their home had no eyes at all. Only the fugitives, the creatures who crept in from outside to shelter and hide, had eyes. There were not many of them. Few sighted creatures will voluntarily venture into a blind world. It is an adaptation which is almost invariably permanent. An organism which is *temporarily* blind is at a great disadvantage.

And so a million vibrating membranes recorded her coughing and the scuffling of her feet. The smell of her was heavy in the air with her sweating and her fast breath, and the warmth of her, too, was there for the feeling. The creatures of the darkness were very much aware of her as she scuttled through the lacunae of their world.

And they reacted. The heat of her flesh drew them. Where she had passed by, her essence lingered in the thick air, an irresistible bait. She ran so fast that she did not signal her coming very far in advance, but every time she passed from one level to the next she sucked something out of the caverns into the zigzag column behind her. They scratched the stairs and they rustled and clicked, but the sound of their hurry meant nothing to Nita, who was simply running.

Up and up.

The whole collective organism which had grown on the bones of the great tower could feel her, like a crumb stuck in a gullet, an indigestible fragment of gristle alarming an intestine...the kind of thing which, in a human, might begin a nightmare... just as rats in the walls may haunt a home. The multidimensional creature was, in its way, conscious of her. It knew her. Impassively, it gathered itself around her and contained her.

She was very tiny.

As Nita's mental inertia carried her up and up, and began to relax while the panic ebbed away, sensory impressions of a vague character began to seep into her consciousness again.

Her mind lingered in the fringes of wakefulness. She sensed the organism almost as it sensed her. She sensed the whole being as a unit, as a crouching beast.

She had no destination. There was no meaning in her frenetic action. She had lost the past and the future was a blank wall pressing against her face, in which there was no moment save the one where she was trapped. Time was not passing. Nothing changed, everything was still, constant. The furious effort by which she hurled herself along and up was nothing—merely a steady leakage of energy from her system. As though her lifeblood was flowing steadily away through an open wound, pumped out pulse by pulse with the beating of her faithful heart.

But she went higher, and still higher. Ultimately, unless the edifice extended forever...even beyond the Face of Heaven, she had to reach the top.

43.

In the meantime, Iorga's situation was not very different. She moved, and he lay still. Otherwise....

His heart beat steadily, and the blood leaked slowly away from his abdomen. Very slowly, mingling as it ran with the acid juices of his stomach, which was ruptured.

He hovered on the borderline between consciousness and unconsciousness. He was not wholly aware of the insects which settled on his skin and crawled into the crevices of his clothing. In time, they would use him up: suck out his juices and lay their eggs by the million in his rotting flesh, but for now they were waiting, letting him die in his own time. However, while his awareness of reality was slight, his mind was still active and there was a strange clarity in his thoughts, a definition about his ideas and images which was unusual. He felt little enough pain, though he knew that it would be a brief respite before the burning in his belly as his lights began to dissolve. That would come, in its own time, and dragging death somewhere behind it.

The gun was in his hand, and it would not have been beyond his power to raise its barrel into his mouth and fire through his brain, but he really could not remember whether there was a bullet left. In any case, the mental image which he still carried of Randal Harkanter's head exploding stood between himself and any such action. The pain would mean little enough to him when it came, and he was content to live with it, for a little while.

He felt that he was dying rather easily.

He knew, somehow, that it should not have been so simple. A couple of cuts with a rough-hewn knife wielded by a savage should not be sufficient to destroy a man like himself. He felt that if the need were more urgent he could shrug off this mortal lassitude, and bring life back into himself by the energy of will. He felt that he still had the power to refuse death. This once, and perhaps several times more. But that power was blocked by an overwhelming indifference—a sense of loss. The creative force that might bring to bear the effort of will and the power of life was not there. The *need* to create was missing.

If Iorga had been an animal, he would have crawled away, and if the predators had not taken advantage of his weakness, he would have survived. There is nothing in an animal except that kind of need.

But Iorga was a man, and between himself and the outside world there was a mind whose decisions were taken according to a whole network of needs and systems. Iorga remembered Aelite, and a long struggle in the Swithering Waste to save her from the cloak-fungus which had grown on her like a cancer. He had that image clear in his mind, and at the same time there were others. The stars in the limitless sky of the Overworld. The blight crawling slowly through the blackland.

There was no doubt in his mind that Nita and Huldi were dead. Intellectually, there had to be doubt, but in his feelings there was none. He felt that it was ended, and so it was.

His life had been emptied of all that it contained, and opened to things it could not and would not contain. And so Iorga allowed himself to die.

44.

Nita, disgorged by a circular aperture that growth-upon-growth of fungus had not managed to close in thousands of years, stood on flat roof, in the middle of a metal-railed arena, with a hundred thousand ghost-moths startled into the fluttering flight of clamoring alarm making a living halo about the crown of the tower. Likewise, a hundred thousand thoughts hovered in the margins of her startled consciousness. The running was finished, the panic dead, and while her heart roared and rattled in a futile attempt to pay back the energy debt owed by her muscles in her limbs, she felt a sudden tremendous sense of presence. Aliveness surged inside her like sunlight.

She had never been so close to the stars. Not one of her ancestors, back to the beginning of consciousness, nor their cousins, had ever come so close to the bleak inner face of the world above, the higher world, the world which engulfed her own.

From where she stood now the stars were each as large as the face of the moon which the heaven-born knew. And they shone so brilliantly white, so completely composed of pure radiance, so steady and so secure. There were ten, or twenty, drawn in a great flat arc across the sky whose black solidity was so close that she felt almost able to feel its metal coldness. Beyond those few, in either direction, they began to blur, to distort, until—ultimately—they faded into a thick line declining to either horizon. Even from a height such as this, she could see no end to the road of stars, in either direction. There was no dead end, and there was no marriage with a radiant horizon. The road of stars was simply swallowed up by the darkness in the maw of the curved world.

She went to the rail, staggering like a corpse whose brain has somehow failed to understand the message of mortality carried by its servant nerves. She dropped the knife, the better to grip

the metal cylinder with her tiny hands. She looked up, and out...
and then down.

She was seized by intense vertigo, and her mind was abruptly
spun into a gyroscopic whirl. She tried to snatch herself back
from the lip of the abyss, but her hands were convulsed, the
ligaments frozen and unyielding, and she was sealed to the rail.
She shut her eyes tight, and tried to gain control of the electrical
turbulence in her brain.

Only when she had fainted did her hands let go and leave
her lying in the gutter, protected by the raised edge of the roof.
She lived for a few moments with the giddy madness of herself
before awareness began to return.

She realized then that tiny clawed feet were swarming all
over her, that a living wave had spilled out of the aperture in
her wake as, once, she had seen a great worm evert its gut over
one of her companions in the Swithering Waste. A living vomit,
coppery in color, bright as though burnished in the brilliant
light of the beautiful stars, was pouring on to her body, rushing
at her from the mouth of the great beast.

She tried to regain her feet, but it was hopeless.

The centipedes clung to her, wrapped themselves around her
limbs, her neck, dangled from her hair. They were innumerable,
and many were several feet in length. They were eyeless, but
their heads roamed ceaselessly, the jaws moving with frantic
eagerness as the palps guided them to flesh into which they
spewed their poison. They covered her, and they covered one
another, the heads perpetually burrowing while the myriad
legs and the long, segmented bodies writhed like gorgon's hair
around her.

45.

Julea was sitting up in bed, listening to music. On the opposite wall film of birds in flight filled an area some eight or ten
feet square. The music and the film were unconnected—there

was no attempt to synchronize or symbolize. The music was a somber symphony, muted and leisurely. The birds were mostly gulls, soaring on cliff-face updrafts. The combination might have been restful, almost sedative, but Joth found somehow that it conflicted with his mood. It annoyed rather than soothed. Looking at Julea, however, he was uncertain of its effect on her. She seemed completely diffident.

She had hardly reacted when he had come into the room. It seemed to make no impression whatsoever on her state of mind. It was as if a stone were dropped into a viscous liquid: a brief stir of recognition, a turgid ripple of attention, and then relapse into quietude.

Ravelvent had warned him in advance that it would not be easy. According to Ravelvent, Julea was emotionally bankrupt. She had stopped caring. She was content simply to live on, without investing anything of herself in anything which might happen or offer itself.

"It's settled now," said Joth, gently. "It's all over. I'm sorry it couldn't end when you wanted it to end, but now it's finished. There's nothing more."

"No," she said, absently. Her eyes were following a gull round and around in long, slow arcs.

"At last," said Joth, "they're beginning to understand. They're beginning to see the need to understand, and they're beginning to want to understand. What my father wanted to do...it's just beginning now."

"It was all because of him," she said. "All of this. If only he'd taken his sleeping pills...." She laughed, faintly, at the irony.

Joth was pleased to see the reaction.

"And no one would have cared," said Joth. "No one would have done anything...until the platform collapsed."

"In a thousand years...," she murmured.

"Our children's children's children," said Joth. "But that's what the Movement stood for. That's what our civilization meant...the willingness of men to protect the future instead of the present, the surrender of personal objectives to the objec-

tives of the race. Isn't that what we were taught to believe in—
isn't that what they tried to force us to believe in? And we do
believe it...but only in our heads. It's only an idea, a rule of the
game we play...."

He paused. She said nothing—he had completely lost her
attention again.

"What are you going to do?" he asked her, his voice sharp-
ening a little to cut into her isolation.

"When?" she said, turning briefly to look at him again.

"When you get out of bed," said Joth. "And after that. What
are you going to do...ever?"

"Stay here," she replied.

"With Ravelvent?"

"Abram," she corrected him.

He shrugged. "He has something against me. Not just what
happened to you...there's some other reason why he doesn't like
me. Do you know why?"

She didn't answer. Instead, she said: "What are you going to
do?"

"Work."

"In the Underworld?"

"Sometimes. A great many people will have to work in the
Underworld for periods of time. Maintenance of the platform's
supporting structures is only a part of it—the easy part. Contact
with the people is something else. That will take time, and it
won't be easy."

"And that's what you want to do?"

"I want to work on the project which will grow out of what
Burstone was doing. I wonder what happened to Burstone...they
questioned him, I know, but there was never any mention of a
trial. I think they must have let him go. He might be useful to
the new Hegemony."

"He tried to kill you."

Joth shook his head. "I'm not sure," he said.

The music finished, and for a few moments the gulls flew
on in a dead, unnatural silence. Then Julea reached out to the

selector panel beside her, and another piece began to play.

Joth nodded toward the film, and said: "How long does this go on for?"

She smiled, very slightly. "It's synthesized," she said. "A basic pattern, repeated with variations. Almost infinite. It can go on forever...just as long as we watch, and our children, and our children's children...."

Joth stared at the images of the birds. There seemed to be so many. It all seemed so real. But on the wall, it was only a pattern of light. With the faculties of the cybernet, there was no reason why a pattern of light should be any more than that. A computer simulation. No more limit to its scope than real gulls flying near real cliffs had limits to *their* scope. The gulls on the film, even though made of light, could dive for fish, could mate, could lay eggs, could fall prey to hawks. But why should they? They could fly forever, if they wanted to.

"Are there others like that?" asked Joth. "Ones with people? Are there whole catalogues full of pattern-of-light people who can be put up on the screen and then set in motion forever, living pattern-of-light lives?"

She shook her head. "It only works with things like gulls," she said. "When it's people, it becomes absurd."

"I wonder why," he said, drily.

He watched the wheeling birds in silence, for a few more minutes. He was quite fascinated.

"I never saw anything like that before," he said.

"It's always been available," she told him. "The net can do so many things...you simply don't realize."

"No."

The music suddenly swelled into a loud, dramatic sequence. For a moment, the music seemed to be carrying the birds. Then it died away again, but the birds were still there, drifting and darting on the unreal air currents.

Suddenly—almost absurdly—Joth thought of Enzo Ulicon. He almost laughed, but then lost the humor of the juxtaposition of ideas as he realized why the image had come into his mind.

Trying to put it into words, he drew Julea's attention with a quick gesture of the hand.

"For the last few days," he said, speaking slowly, feeling his way, "I've been trying to convince Eliot Rypeck and Enzo Ulicon that they must stop the plan to destroy the Underworld. I talked to them endlessly, and in the end, I went through a kind of experiment, trying to make contact with someone or something in the Underworld, to prove that such a contact could be made, and was only an extension of the kind of thing which is already happening in our dreams.

"When all that was over, Ulicon questioned me. I thought...I was convinced...that he was trying as hard as anyone possibly could to find out exactly what had happened, and how, and why. But when it was over...when he'd asked the questions he had to ask...he just switched off. Just like *that*. All of a sudden, he began talking and thinking about something quite different— Heres' removal and Dayling's takeover. And the way he talked, and what he said, suddenly seemed to me to be so utterly child-like, so completely detached from reality.

"I suppose I might have seen the same thing a hundred times before, but that particular moment I was completely wrapped up in what I'd been trying to do, trying to understand and to remember and to evaluate. I thought he was, too. I thought that what we were saying and doing was vitally important. But it wasn't—not to him. He just wasn't involved with it... not really. When he wanted to, he could deliberately involve himself—throw himself into the problem—but he could just as easily disassociate himself again. And that, just at that moment, appalled me. I just couldn't see *how*....

"But I think I do, now. Perhaps. I think I may have been just the same, once, but what happened to me in the Underworld changed me. Permanently. It wiped out the person there used to be, and made a new one, and even coming back to the machine and the i-minus drug couldn't change me back again.

"You see, to Ulicon, reality is just patterns of light. It's all superficial, all a matter of appearances. There's no difference, so far as he's concerned, between those gulls on the wall and real ones. The quality of his experience is precisely the same in either case. But I feel a difference. I don't *see* it, in the film, but I feel it.

"And...as you say...I can't help feeling that when it's people, it's absurd."

She looked at him blankly. She had not even tried to follow the argument. It would have been no use if she had.

"It's just that...he doesn't seem to live inside his head. He lives...inside the machine. The cybernet's senses are more important than his own."

As the words drained away, he looked into her eyes. He tried to look through them, into her mind. He tried to see what she was thinking. But he couldn't. Her life, like Ulicon's, like Ravelvent's, like all the rest, was contained in the four walls which enclosed her and the electronic brain which made them what they were.

46.

The roofs of gleaming silver, domed and arched, peaked and tented, stretched endlessly away into the distance. Sunlight glittered in windows scattered like flotsam over the rippled surface. In grooves and slits, and over threads and bridges, moved tiny vehicles. Like ants in a hill, they seemed integral parts of a great system, whose logic and strategy was too vast, too god-like, for the entities themselves even to suspect.

The sim hovered near the spires of the western extreme of the complex, tinting them with red and casting dappled shadows in the furthest streets. The room in which Dayling stood was circular, its windows curved. It was easy to forget the direction of weight, provided only that he stood very still, and lost himself in the illusion that the world was tilting this way and that, the gleaming complex spinning like a great metal plate, with himself as its center, and his vantage its cockpit.

Dayling was not afraid of falling. He was master of the illusion. He felt, in this particular moment, that he was master of the sky as of the city, and that the thin, languid clouds were his to command.

This was a city—one of several cities on the face of the Earth—but it was a city where no one lived. Men worked here, in their thousands, each of them engaged in the basic task of instructing the machines, but the city was *for* and *of* machines. No one lived in cities—cities were held to be unfit for human habitation. Houses stood alone. The cities were the organs of the cybernet.

This particular organ was the brain. It was the largest, the most complex, and the most vital. It was here, in Euchronia's brain, that the personality of Euchronia was determined, that the thoughts of the human race happened, that the self-awareness of the human race was contained.

Dayling looked out from the crown of Euchronia's steel skull, and rejoiced in being, now—and perhaps for a long time to come—the *idée fixe* within that brain. The dominant idea... the delusion of grandeur.

The mundane functions of the Euchronian organism went on as they had under Heres, and under the kingpins of a thousand other Euchronian councils. The hunger of the race was satiated, the thirst, the need to rest, to excrete, to receive occasional stimuli of excitation. Even the sense of identity which the brain of Euchronia possessed was very little affected. The body was the same, and the face. Its state of health was not changed.

In a way, the alteration which had taken place was the most trivial possible. Only the very highest, most abstract functions of the brain and mind of Euchronia had been affected. What had taken place was a kind of religious conversion, a sudden reinvestment in a new set of ideas, a sudden rediscovery of purpose and ambition.

But Dayling felt all the triumph, all the exultancy which such a conversion inevitably brings. He felt the power, and the pleasure. He felt the confidence of the newly faithful—the confidence that the great organism whose brain contained him was *immortal*, and *ultimately meaningful.*

To him, these concepts went hand in hand, inseparable, just as they had to Heres, and to the first Euchronians. But Dayling, it will be remembered, was a mortal man. Like the patterns of electric discharge forever forming and decaying within his own brain, he was transient...a ghost in the machine.

He was thinking, as he looked out over the glistening panorama of his power: "Now is the time to build, to clear away the sterile ideas of the Movement and build a real world...a world adapted to mankind...a perfect world. We have the instrument, if only we have the mind...."

47.

There was Festival in Cynabel, in the heartland of Shairn. More than twenty thousand people were in the town and the fields around: fields to which the blight had not yet come but which were stripped bare nevertheless. Even so, of twenty thousand people more than half were starving.

Only a fraction of the vast assembly could gather before the long house for the Festival. Cynabel was a large town, by Shairan standards, but refugees from the north had swollen its numbers eightfold. Thousands more might be in the marshes and the bare hills, but they too would have to travel southward as the blight came.

The crowd around the throne-stone had never been so vast nor so dense—and perhaps never so quiet. They waited anxiously, desperately, not so much for the confrontation with their Gray Souls, but because they were in dire need of guidance from the priests, from the wise men, from the strong men, and from the prophets. They had to be told what to do. Their lives—their whole way of life—was being eaten out from beneath them. In such a time, prophets are needed. They are more necessary than any other breed of men.

The Shaira had confidence in their prophets, for they knew them to be more intimately in contact with the Gray Souls than other men, and they had implicit faith in their Souls.

Chemec the crab stood close by the throne-stone, waiting. Of all men in Shairn he was, at this moment, the most important. His greatness had been thrust upon him by chance, by the Souls, and by the priests. He was a puppet to all these things, and he was the focal point of the destiny of Shairn.

The drums beat with the slow, steady rhythm which all men knew. The beat was no louder, but it seemed, perhaps, a little *larger.* There was something massive in the way the sound swelled and spread about the town. The drummers were beside the long house, and in the shadow of the earthen wall. They were Cynabel's drummers, but they were also Kerata's and Myrmeleon's, Asica's and Fiera's, and others from the north and the east. When the horns blew, they seemed to fill the air and the land with mournful crying—the wailing of Shairn.

There was not one fire, but fifty, each confined within a ring of stone and huddled round with silent people. The embers burned red and spat sparks, and no flames danced in them. No smoke clouded the air.

Only a fraction of the assembly possessed enough of the leaf-like fronds from which the pulp used in the festival derived. The small, lichenous plant had suffered from the blight as had everything else. For the rest—rather more than half—this would be a barren Festival in terms of spiritual comfort.

The elders, the Chemec with them, stood with eyes closed, absorbing the rhythm of the drums and the strange cadence of the horns, reaching for the inner sight, as always, without the aid of the pulp. They would contact their Souls, because they had faith. The others, used to the crutch provided by the drug, would not.

There was no clear space around the throne stone for the dance of the Star King. On this occasion, the ritual would be practiced in another fashion. There was to be no transfer of power, no death. This was to be a Festival without secular leaders. The robes which the priests wore had one sleeve black with sequins of silver, the other golden yellow. Each one, therefore, had taken into himself the roles of sun and stars.

The pace of the drums grew slower and slower, and the metabolism of each of the listeners, attuned to the rhythm, began to slow down. The crying of the horns melted into the low beat, and became almost constant—the notes tortured, dragged into indefinite extension.

When the moment finally came, Chemec was very calm inside himself. His senses were relaxed, and he was in a light trance. The power which took hold of his voice was not under his conscious control, but it was nevertheless his voice and not that of the Gray Soul within him. He knew what he had to say, and as long as it was said, it did not matter what power guided the words: his, or the Soul's, or the elders'. The message was the same.

He told the people that Shairn was dying. He told them that they must leave Shairn, and go west-of-south, into the lands where the Men Without Souls lived. They would not be welcome, and the journey would be hard, because the Men Without Souls were poor farmers, and lived mostly out of the wilds. The Children of the Voice, too, would have to live on the wild country, and they would have to fight, even to do that. The Ahriman horde which had passed through Shairn had also gone into that country, and it might be that the Shaira would have to face the Ahrima a second time.

For the Children of the Voice, said Chemec, there would always be war, wherever they moved. But the Children of the Voice would win, because they would move together, in an army so vast as to be unconquerable. They would live like Ahrima, but they would not die so fast, because they had more to sustain them in life.

He told them that this was not a matter of invasion. They could not and would not try to take the lands into which they moved in order to settle there. They would have to move on, and on, because the blight which killed Shairn would follow them wherever they went, and though they would stay ahead of its relentless march it would always be moving, always behind them.

They must keep going, he said, while they died, and while their children died, and while their children's children died. No one would see the end of the march, nor would their children.

And then began the prophecy:

Though Shairn died now, it would not die forever. Though all that lived was perishing of the blight, new life would spring up again. In time, the new life would spread throughout the land, and make it good again. So, too, would all the dead lands flower and flourish once again, in their turn.

There would be a time, he promised, that the Children of the Voice would return to Shairn. They would not find their villages and their homes, but they would find new life throughout the land. Though no man living and listening would ever see his homeland again, the children of his children's children's children would return, and find it a new home, and make it once again the land called Shairn.

Before then, there would be hardship. Though thousands would begin the journey, and tens of thousands, perhaps only hundreds would return. Some, no doubt, would be lost on the way, and might live on in other lands, as different people. But the true people of Shairn would be guided, not by Chemec, who must die, but by their Souls, and by the hero Camlak, killer of the Harrowhound, who had seen Heaven. The people of Shairn would be one people, and they would come home one people, in due time, no matter how many or how few lived, no matter how many or how few went their own way.

Thus Chemec gave to the people of Shairn not only a purpose, a goal, and hope, but also an identity, and a unity. He was a prophet, and he gave them a saint: a dead hero, who lived nevertheless, who was both guardian and guide to the Shaira.

Those who saw, during that Festival, their Gray Souls knew that what Chemec said was true. But even those who did not— those without the pulp or the inner strength—*believed*. When the great trek began, there was no one who stayed behind. A handful, perhaps, could have scraped a living out of what the blight left, might even have protected some tiny area from the blight, driving it out with fire as some of the northern villages had tried to do, with limited success. But no one chose to try. When the twenty thousand left Cynabel, and became thirty and forty thousand while they passed through the remaining villages and towns of Shairn, none stayed behind them. All followed, secure in the knowledge that one day, in some manner, the children of their children's children's children would bring the name of Shairn back to the reborn land.

48.

Having failed to make contact with Rafael Heres through the medium of the cybernet, Eliot Rypeck sat back in quiet contemplation. There was, he supposed, every reason why Heres should not be accepting calls, especially from himself.

Rypeck knew full well that Heres would consider himself betrayed, and he was not at all sure that he did not agree. He *had* betrayed such trust as Heres had put in him. He had released not only the secret of the i-minus project, but also the news concerning the corrosion of the pillars. In so doing, Rypeck had dealt a death blow to the Euchronian Movement as a political monopoly. And in going further, committing himself to the new government under Dayling, he had—almost entirely by his own action—destroyed the Movement even as a political entity.

And the pity of it all was that Eliot Rypeck still believed in Euchronianism. He still believed that there could be a Millennium, if only the right historical route could be discovered, and if only the right social evolution could take place. Rypeck still wanted *everybody* to win. But he had come to believe in Euchronia for all the people of Earth, not just Euchronia for the Euchronians. The strength of his faith had made him into a heretic, as strength of faith always tends to do.

He could not help feeling a kind of relief at the fact that he had been unable to reach Heres. He had felt it his duty to try—to face the man he had deposed, and be accused—but he had not really known what he could say, or whether there was anything to be said at all. The gulf which had now opened up between himself and the ex-Hegemon was not something which could be healed, by words, by time, by any human action. Rypeck had smeared Heres' image of the world, and nothing could cancel that.

Rypeck felt sorry for Heres, and he also felt shame in himself. But he stood by what he had done. If, in time, it was proved to be a mistake, he would still stand by it. He did not lack trust in himself. For a moment, though, while he thought of Heres, he wished that all that had happened could be wiped out, cut away from the thread of history, and the clock turned back so that all the choices might be taken again, by wiser men.

Then he put Heres out of his mind.

Much later, he discovered that the reason he had failed to make contact was that Heres had hanged himself.

49.

When Warnet came back to see him a second time, Sisyr was feeling a great deal better in himself. The pain had been controlled, new growth was replacing the destroyed tissues.

They had taken the bullets out of him, because they dared not leave them inside. The surgeons had been very much afraid, in performing the operation, that through ignorance they might kill the alien rather than helping him, but they had been even more afraid that the same result might accrue through inaction. Sisyr knew that what they had done was neither dangerous nor necessary, but he understood, in his mind, the conflict which must have taken place in *their* minds. He was grateful for their decision.

He had been in pain for some considerable time, and he had

slept deeply while much of the internal repair work had been carried out. But this was simply an incident that had to be lived through, and he had been content to live through it, allowing it to take the time it took without anxiety or any other kind of mental turmoil. Warnet had tried to talk to him before, and had found communication difficult. Now, however, all was well again...or becoming well again.

"Burstone went into one of the Sanctuaries," said Warnet. "If and when he decides to return, he will be isolated."

"It is not necessary," replied the alien.

"Why did he shoot you?"

"I think," said the alien, "that you might call it a lack of instinct. His mind was altered by changing circumstance, and it had no...capacity to steer. The action was a product of the distortion. It was futile, without meaning."

"He meant to kill you."

"Yes—but it does not matter."

Warnet stared for a while at the inhuman face, still finding it strange to his eyes, though he had looked into it so many times before.

"What will you do now?" he asked. "Will you stay, or will you leave us to our miserable inheritance? We can't really protect you."

"If you will let me," said the alien, "I will stay."

"Why?"

"This is my home."

Warnet eased forward. "You once told me that you had no secrets. But you do. Perhaps you are not absolutely determined to conceal things from us, but there are things which are concealed, nevertheless. Will you reveal those things, if I ask you?"

"I will tell you anything I can," said Sisyr.

"The trouble is," said the Eupsychian, "that I'm not quite sure what it is that I want to know. I can only ask you again: why do you stay here on Earth?"

Sisyr considered the question. Eventually, he said: "You

understand, I think, why that is such a difficult question. I do not think as you do. My reasons would not necessarily sound like reasons to you. The way I see reality and the way you see it are not the same. Obviously, you would consider it frivolous if I were simply to say that I have to live somewhere—here, or on another world—and that I am here. You would want to know whether I might not find it more pleasant living with others of my kind. I would not. It is, in fact, necessary that I live apart from others of my own kind. We...meet...occasionally, and that is good. But we cannot stay together. We are, by nature, solitary."

"Shall I tell you why I think you are here on Earth?" asked Warnet.

"It may make things easier," said the alien. "Or more difficult."

Warnet smiled. "I think you are here because Earth is your experiment. I know that for many centuries you have been observing life in the Underworld, and I think that during the same period of time you have been observing the Overworld also. Discreetly, of course, with the help of the machine you helped to create.

"I think you are—playing Hoh. I think you understand what I mean by that. Perhaps even playing god. I think you came to Earth in the beginning because you were looking for it, and I think you stay because you are still looking. You are waiting for something to happen—something which is important to you by virtue of what you are."

"There is truth, of a kind, in what you say," said Sisyr. "You see me, perhaps, as a lonely wanderer adrift in the universe, searching for some ideal...a holy grail. And perhaps that is what I am. But there is a flaw in that idea, just as there is a flaw in every analogy you might draw. You think, you see, in finite terms. You think of experiments and results, of searches and goals. You know that I am immortal, and you see this planet as a stage in my life, something with a beginning and an end. A game of Hoh reaches a conclusion—inevitably, for that is the kind of game it is. The conclusions may be widely various, but there is always an end-point of some kind. In all your games there is some state which you play *toward*.

"All the games that my people play are infinitely extended in time. There is never beginning, and never end, but only change. I am involved in the quality and nature of eternal change, whereas you—an ephemeral being—are concerned with abstractions from that change.

"You have a concept called infinity, but you are not infinite. Your infinity is a logical artifact. Mine is a reality. You cannot discover an end or a beginning to time—so far as you can imagine, the universe always has existed and always will. But you experience duration as finite. There was a time before you existed, and there will be a time after you are dead. You accept this, but you do not experience it. That is your nature.

"By virtue of your nature, you cannot comprehend mine. I do not wish to claim that I understand yours—perhaps the way I see you is only a logical artifact. But you must be able to accept the idea that what time is to me is not what time is to you. And because time is different, so is space. And because space is different, so is the very nature of existence.

"I will offer you another analogy. You are a three-dimensional being. I am a four-dimensional being. What you see of me is only a cross-section through me. You perceive me as an actor in your reality, an actor who can interact meaningfully with you on your terms. But there is more to me than that. I can attempt to simulate your kind of consciousness, and succeed—to some extent. I am not sure whether you can attempt to simulate mine. Perhaps not.

"You ask me: why am I here? What is your world to me? I can only begin to make an answer.

"Your scientists have put a great deal of effort into the extension of the human life-span. That research shows results—you might expect to live twice or three times as long as your prehistoric forefathers. Your social philosophers—most especially the Euchronians, but also the Eupsychians, to a lesser extent—have embraced similar aims: they have tried to design and make societies with longer life-spans, for the long-lived people. You have always fought for stability, because in stability you see the antidote to death.

"But even within your own people, there has always been a dissenting voice—or its echo—which holds that a longer, more stable lifetime is not—and cannot be—any richer in experience than a shorter, less stable one. I do not wish to say that this dissenting voice contains the truth, because your truth is not my truth, and I cannot judge. But consider my viewpoint.

"I am not merely long-lived, but eternal—if I so choose. I can accept death if I wish, and many of my people do. We are a declining race, ever becoming fewer. You may find an irony in that—the idea of an immortal race dwindling slowly into extinction. But this is so. The reason is stability. Once life becomes stable, it becomes empty—that is what we think and that is what we *feel*. Those of us who elect to die do so because of an overwhelming feeling that they have exhausted life, that it has nothing more to offer them, and that it is pointless to continue.

"You think that I came to Earth in search of something. I came in search of instability. But you will, perhaps, be able to understand that instability is not a goal, in the sense that you have goals. In searching for instability, it is not enough to find... one has to keep on finding, forever. The discovery has to be made over and over again, with each new day and each new year. For me and my people, it is not enough that the universe should be infinite in extent, either in time or in space. It must also be infinite in *experience*—for otherwise, how can we find a purpose in our infinite lives? Perhaps there is no such purpose. Perhaps we are doomed to failure in the search for it. Perhaps, in a million or a million million of your lifetimes, we will all have chosen mortality, and died. But in the meantime...the effort continues.

"My kind have lived so much longer in the universe than yours that you find it almost inconceivable that we have little more scientific knowledge than you. When your people have lately come to me demanding help, they have taken it for granted that any miracle they could ask, I could perform. It is not so. My kind have no more scientific knowledge now than we had billions of years ago, because we found that science had very little to offer us beyond the tools to move about the universe. Beyond that, we found science an embarrassment. Science, you see, is founded upon the basic assumption that the universe is an ordered and systematic place, whose principles of organization are both rational and comprehensible. But what good was that assumption to us? What *we* needed was not science, but anti-science. We needed to proceed on the exactly opposite assumption that the universe was *not* wholly ordered— that there was an element of irrationality. Without that element of irrationality, you see, there could be no ultimate escape from stability.

"We had to abandon religion as well as science, for the fundamental assumption there is not so very different—it argues rationality but incomprehensibility. The last god which my people worshipped, so very long ago, was an insane god. There seemed to be no other trust that we could place in a god beyond the hope that he was insane. But we find too much rationality to believe in such a deity. Our best hope seems to be the flaw underlying scientific philosophy, a wholly secular belief that beneath the facade of reason and natural law the universe, in the final analysis, does not make sense.

"I think that you may be able to see, now, what I am doing on Earth. It is, if you like, my experiment—an attempt to test my belief. But you will notice that it is an experiment that can only fail. If it succeeds, it proves nothing beyond the fact that I can continue.

"I helped your people to build the Overworld, knowing that it would fail...ultimately. I helped to make the Underworld what it is: a cauldron of evolutionary turmoil, where change is near to its most extreme. I will confess to you now that I contributed to that change by genetic engineering. The Children of the Voice are a collaboration between myself and chance, just as the Overworld is a collaboration between myself and order. In the end, I *must* believe, chance and change will win. They cannot be defeated. They must win, not only on Earth, but *everywhere*.

"Having said that, I must risk your anger. This, you will say, is interference...I have been intruding into the substance of your lives, threatening the very pattern of your existence. You may, perhaps, feel that what I have done—what I am doing—is evil. But I must say this: that I am dealing with factors which belong to a far greater time-scale than the one by which you live your lives. What I have done is negligible, in your terms. *Your* quest for stability is a purely temporary thing. You can find stability, if that is what you want, within a historical pattern which, from my viewpoint, is eternally chaotic. Because you ask so little, you have every chance of success. Because you are so transient, you have the opportunity to make whatever you want out of your lives: you do not have my limitations.

"Perhaps you will be unable to understand what it is that I have been trying to achieve here on Earth. I do not know that there is any way I can tell you which will help you to understand, because it is something which has virtually no meaning so far as you are concerned. But I will say it this way: what I have sought to gain from Earth is a glimpse of infinity—some hint of evidence that the universe is not only infinite in size, but infinite in incident. I have tried to find something new, in pursuit of the faith that there is *always* something new...something beyond. Beyond the shape and form of the universe there has to be shapelessness and formlessness, and there had to be a way to see and to know that chaos here on Earth. That is what the Children of the Voice mean to me: they may give me a glimpse of infinity.

"Perhaps I should add just one more thing, with reference to that point, and it is this: for you, too, what has happened and is happening may provide a window into new possibilities. Your people, unlike mine, have so many choices, so many opportunities. But here are more, opening up before you.

"You cannot know how much I envy you."

50.

The road went over the edge of the world. Joth braked, and got out. He went to the brink of the Overworld, and looked down, following the sweep of the highway as it slanted down the metal face in a vast, shallow arc. The face was concave—headlands to north and south carried spurs of the overworld out beyond the expanse of sandy beach, and only dissolved into irregular masses of bare black rock some way out to sea. But the road curved out and looped back on itself, disappearing into a black semicircle cut out of the steel cliff.

The sun was setting into the sea, its light turning the sea gold and the hazed air pink. The great wall which enclosed the Underworld was fiery with reflected glare. Joth watched the garish display until the sun was gone and the colors began to drown. He knew that the afterglow would last for a long time, and even when he looked back over his shoulder to the eastern horizon, he could see no stars. Nor was there a moon.

He went back to the car, and drove it over the edge of the world, following the long decline. There were no seabirds—they found the metal cliffs too inhospitable. Seabirds lived almost entirely on uninhabited offshore islands—miniature sanctuaries.

Gradually, the sky darkened, and he switched on the headlights of the car. Cut into the saline dirt which had been deposited on the road over a great many years he could see the imprints left by Germont's ill-fated convoy not so very long ago.

When he reached the bottom, he switched off the lights and got out of the car again. He did not drive into the tunnel. He did not even look at the tunnel, at first, but walked off the causeway on to the sand, and looked out over the sea. The weed and detritus which marked the last high tide was only thirty or forty feet from the edge of the road, and he walked out to stir the stinking wrack with his feet. Tiny crustaceans squirmed in the wet sand he exposed. He looked at them, and wondered which of Earth's two worlds they belonged to: the old, or the new. Perhaps they, and everything within the ocean, were part of a third world, neither old nor new, neither Under nor Over— an eternal womb of life undisturbed by magnificent Plans and huge steel follies.

Overhead, the stars began to shine through. The night was cloudless, and they shone in their thousands. Behind him, his footprints, imprinted in the wet sand, gradually filled up with water, and their edges began to crumble. The footmarks lost their shape, and became mere puddles. He walked on a little way, toward the sea, looking for small pools held by the rippled sand and the thin ridges of rock. But the loneliness and the darkness quickly became oppressive, and he turned back.

From the back of the car he collected a heavy flashlight, and armed with this he directed his attention to the tunnel into the Underworld.

Curiously, although this was undoubtedly the end-point of the road of stars, there seemed to be no light in the great corridor for the first few hundred yards. Without the beam of the torch, he could see nothing in the tunnel except the merest gleam of distant light. There was nothing that might attract a man—or even an animal—into its depths. From *inside*, though, the red glow of the setting sun might be clearly visible during certain seasons.

Joth walked into the tunnel mouth, playing the light of his torch all around and up above. He did not go far. He intended to wait—perhaps sitting in the car—for an hour or two, and then drive away. He would return, at the same time of day, in a few days' time, and he would continue to return again and again, until something happened, or until he became convinced that nothing ever would. He had chosen evening, and the hours that followed twilight, because he knew that people waiting within would only venture out after the sun was gone.

But these intentions were not necessary. He did not have to wait, because someone was already there, waiting for him. She came to him cautiously, with her weapon drawn, because she could not see him while he stood behind the light, and she could not be sure that it was him. But she allowed herself to be caught by the beam, so that he could see her.

Only when he spoke, saying "Huldi!", did she know for certain who it was.

He questioned her. She told him all she knew about Iorga and Nita—the encounter with the Cuchumanates...her fall...and her recovery to find herself alone. She had not dared to go into the building in search of the others. She had waited outside until she was sure that they were not coming. She had killed the last of the Cuchumanates with her knife.

And she had followed the road of stars to its ultimate end.

Joth led her outside, and showed her the stars in the sky. But she was so frightened by the ocean and the towering metal face, and the illimitable depth of the sky, that she really saw very little. Iorga had seen so much more, and Nita, if only she had lived....

But the merest glimpse of infinity was, to Huldi, a terrifying thing.

She would not get into the car, and so they went back into the tunnel, together. He asked her what she would do now, and she could not tell him. She had not thought, but had merely followed the road to its end. He wanted to take her to another part of the world, to deliver her into lands which were lighted by many stars, where people of her own kind lived, but there was no way that he could do that. The only way she would go was back, into the blacklands. He told her to go south rather than following the road east, because his map assured him that there were lighted lands that way, and not too far distant. He gave her the flashlight. Whether she would take his advice, he did not know. She said she would go south, but he did not know whether she was telling the truth.

Before they parted, they made love—for the second time.

51.

The sentence of exile which Heres had passed on Sisyr was confirmed, and he left Earth. He never returned.

52.

In time, all Chemec's prophecies came true.

ABOUT THE AUTHOR

Brian Stableford was born in Yorkshire in 1948. He taught at the University of Reading for several years, but is now a full-time writer. He has written many science-fiction and fantasy novels, including *The Empire of Fear, The Werewolves of London, Year Zero, The Curse of the Coral Bride, The Stones of Camelot,* and *Prelude to Eternity.* Collections of his short stories include a long series of *Tales of the Biotech Revolution,* and such idiosyncratic items as *Sheena and Other Gothic Tales* and *The Innsmouth Heritage and Other Sequels.* He has written numerous nonfiction books, including *Scientific Romance in Britain, 1890-1950; Glorious Perversity: The Decline and Fall of Literary Decadence; Science Fact and Science Fiction: An Encyclopedia;* and *The Devil's Party: A Brief History of Satanic Abuse.* He has contributed hundreds of biographical and critical articles to reference books, and has also translated numerous novels from the French language, including books by Paul Féval, Albert Robida, Maurice Renard, and J. H. Rosny the Elder.